G GEMIN

First published in the UK in 2014 by Nosy Crow Ltd
The Crow's Nest, 10a Lant Street
London, SE1 1QR, UK

1 3 5 7 9 10 8 6 4 2

A CIP catalogue record for this book is available from the British Library

Printed and bound in the UK by Clays Ltd, St Ives Plc
Typeset by Tiger Media Ltd, Bishops Stortford, Hertfordshire

Papers used by Nosy Crow are made from wood grown in sustainable forests.

ISBN: 978 0 85763 281 4

www.nosycrow.com

For

Papa, Mamma, Barbara and Joe

One

I was screaming for my life.

It was a mad thing to do – if something was coming the other way I'd be splattered. I felt the wind was going to pull my face off. The handlebars were juddering like I was going a hundred miles an hour, and the wheels sounded like they were screaming too. I squeezed my eyes shut, waiting for the crash.

Then I heard a moo.

I opened my eyes and saw cows in the road – loads of them.

I pulled hard on the brakes and swerved to avoid them, but the handlebars caught a fence post and I flew off the bike. My leg and arm ripped on the road.

I felt stinging pain creeping through my body as I lay there. My helmet had slipped over my eyes, and I could hear the wheel of my bike clicking as it turned. I heard a loud moo, close by. I pulled the helmet off and saw the cows glaring down at me. There's something about a cow's eyes – wild and staring, like they're going to trample you to death. Petrified, I was.

Slowly I began to get up, then one of them started coming for me – it was gigantic.

I screamed again.

"What you screeching about?"

She was standing behind me, like one of the cows had turned into her. It was Cowgirl. You'd never think she was still at school she's so big, let alone Year Eight. She always seems angry too – red cheeks and eyes narrow. No one likes her.

"Get 'em away!" I shouted.

"They're cows not crocodiles," she said. "They won't do you any harm."

She clapped her hands. "C'mon girls. Jane. Rachel. Megan. Away!"

They moved off, just like that – scared of her, most like.

"They shouldn't be on the road," I said, as I got up.

"They're dairy cows, not bulls," said Cowgirl. "And

you were going too fast."

I started having a go at her as I picked up my bike. I suppose I was more embarrassed than angry. Then a woman came out of nowhere. "Hello," she said, smiling at me.

"She fell off her bike," said Cowgirl.

It was her mam, I guessed. "Oh, you've hurt your leg, love," she said to me. "Have you come all this way to see Kate?"

I was cringing, but before I could say anything she was insisting I came into the farmhouse to clean up.

So now I was in Cowgirl's kitchen eating cake and drinking tea after cycling in the cold. It was lovely, but I wondered what Sian would say.

While her mam was seeing to my cuts Cowgirl didn't even look at me. She just sat there staring out the window. Then she got up, said she was going to the shed and walked out.

"She's off to milk the cows," her mam explained as she finished tying the bandage. "Go and watch her if you like."

Well, I could hardly have said I don't like cows or Cowgirl. So I went.

The cows were all waiting patiently to go into the milking shed. Their breath made little puffs of smoke in the cold air. Cowgirl pushed her way through them, like she was shoving aside kids in the school corridor. A couple of the cows gave me the evil eye and I froze.

Cowgirl glanced back at me. "Still scared?"

That annoyed me, so I gritted my teeth and followed her. The cows were as tall as me and wide as a car – massive – and the stink they gave off was rank.

Cowgirl opened a metal gate and the cows followed her in. I kept well back and stood by a big glass tank. The cows went straight to the milking stations, no barging or squabbling, while the others just waited their turn. Cowgirl went round and attached tubes to the udders, one by one. I'd seen it on the telly, like, but in front of you it's different. I couldn't keep my eyes away, to be honest. The pumps sucked the milk along tubes, while the cows ate from a trough in front of them, and then milk started gushing into the tank next to me. It wasn't long before Cowgirl was ready for the next lot. "You wanna put the suckers on?" she asked me.

I didn't have the nerve. "Got to get back."

"Go then," she said.

Rude cow, I thought.

"I will!"

So I left.

Two

I came down the last part of Craig-y-Nos hill without pedalling, eyes open this time. I waited for the bike to slow to a complete stop. No one was around, as if there was nobody left on earth 'cept me. I hadn't found the waterfall place I was looking for so I was fed up.

I got off the bike and lay down in the middle of the road. It was mad, but I was in a mood and didn't want to go home, not straight away.

The road felt hard and cold as I gazed at clouds and the tops of trees above me. I liked the silence – wasn't used to it. When it started to rain I still didn't get up. The raindrops felt cool. My leg and arm throbbed where Cowgirl's mam had patched me up, and I thought about Cowgirl's mad, staring cows. They'd be back in the fields by now and I wondered if they minded the rain.

I heard a car coming down the hill. I should've got up, but after everything that had happened I didn't care. Even as it got nearer and louder I still didn't move. The wheels moaned and groaned as they came to a stop behind me. I heard the car door open.

"You all right?"

A farmer-type was glaring down at me.

"No ... I mean, yes."

I got up. There was something familiar about his face, but he seemed more angry than concerned. As he got back into the truck I picked up my bike and moved out of the way. I watched him drive off, and just as I was about to lie down again my mobile rang. It was Mam.

"Yeah?"

"*Where are you?*"

No way was I going to tell her what I'd been searching for, or that I'd cycled from the top of the valley with my eyes shut and almost got crushed by a herd of cows. "Out on my bike."

"*Ruby's dead,*" she said, like she was telling me

dinner was ready. Ruby was my gran's dog.

"*I said you'd go round and bury it for her.*"

"Oh, Mam! You and Darren are nearer."

"*OK, Gemma, I'll go, shall I? And you can get back here and make dinner with your brother then? You know how much your gran loved that dog...*"

"All right, all right. I'll go!"

I'd been in the countryside, but now it was all concrete and shutters – back on the Bryn Mawr estate after ten minutes' hard pedalling. I live in the new part of the Mawr, which is a big estate stuck on to the old bit. In between is the Bryn Mawr Common, which is covered in litter and bits of furniture. You don't want to live here, I tell you. The old part of the Mawr is a bit nicer. There's rows of terraced streets, where Gran lives, and alleyways that run along the back of them. Gran has a house on one of the terraces. By the time I arrived it was pouring with rain. I went into the backyard. Gran opened the door and gazed up at the grey sky.

"Least it'll make the digging easier," she said, as I stood in front of her getting soaked through.

"Don't ask me in, Gran!"

"Sorry," she said, which made me feel guilty, as she'd just lost her dog – even though I'd never liked it.

As I dug the hole Gran watched from the back window.

"Remember it's got to take the shrub too!" she shouted.

"Yes, Gran!" I was freezing and trying to be patient, but I wanted to get it over with. Gran was the only one who'd liked Ruby, because she was the only person it didn't snarl at or bite. I could feel someone watching me, apart from Gran, and when I glanced up I saw Mr Banerjee staring at me over the wall from next door. He must be ninety, if he's not a hundred, and he's got creepy, bulging eyes.

"Dog dead?" he asked.

I nodded, then the back door to the alley swung open and Jamie Thorpe came in. "S'up, Gemma?"

"Burying Ruby."

"Cool." He stood there in the rain, as if it was a sunny day.

Gran banged on the window. "Get AWAY!"

Jamie ignored her. "Bit me once, that dog did. Had to have a jab."

"Yeah, I remember – Ruby hated having that jab."

"No, me – I had the jab."

He didn't get my sark – bit thick he is.

"C'mon Jamie!" someone called from the alley.

Gran came out into the backyard. "Get away, you little hoodie!"

"Not wearing a hood," Jamie replied.

Gran marched across to me, snatched the shovel out of my hand and turned on him. "You get or I'll be digging a bigger hole."

Jamie stared at her – he just wasn't bothered. So Gran went for him. "You little…" He ducked away just as the shovel crunched on to the doorpost.

"Glad your dog's dead!" he shouted.

Gran slammed the back door closed and turned on me. "Just stand there why don't you!"

"He's not worth it, Gran."

"I can't even bury Ruby in peace. And poor Mave getting burgled only yesterday, while she was in her own home..." Gran raised her arms to the sky. "This place is going to Hell!"

She was losing it, and I was a bit freaked. She went back inside and came out with the dog wrapped in a blanket. I went to take it off her.

"No. I want to do it."

The back-alley door opened again. Gran turned around sharp, but it was Mr Banerjee standing there in his long Indian gown. He stepped forward and laid some flowers on Ruby's body. "For your dog's soul," he said.

That set Gran off crying. "Thank you."

She knelt down and placed Ruby in the hole, taking ages to make sure it wasn't squashed. Mr Banerjee was muttering prayers in Indian, I think, while I just stood there getting soaked.

Gran pointed at the shrub she had bought. I took it to her. She placed it into the hole and pushed the earth all around, pressing it down gently. She stayed on her knees for ages – saying goodbye to Ruby, I guessed. Finally, she stood up with a groan and looked up at the sky. Rain pitter-pattered on her face. Her chin crumpled and she let out a sob. I touched her arm. "Gran?"

She looked at me in a funny way. "Stay and have something to eat with me."

It was like she was begging. I felt sorry for her, so I nodded. Though to be honest, I preferred to eat with Gran than go home.

THREE

Gran's got a lovely real fire. It's one of her "busies" as she calls it. She always says, "*If you don't keep busy, you'll fade and die.*"

I was stoking the fire as Gran came back in. I sneezed.

"Come on, girl. Get yourself upstairs," she said. "Dry yourself and put on one of your granddad's jumpers."

I wasn't going to argue with her in the mood she was in.

It'd been ages since I was in Gran's bedroom. I dried myself down and looked for something to wear. Gran keeps everything. I opened a drawer and there were Granddad's jumpers. I could hardly remember him, but I suddenly felt sad – Gran was clanking around downstairs and Granddad was as dead as Ruby. The jumpers smelled rank, but I wanted to get back to the fire, so I grabbed the top one and pulled it on.

Just before I went I heard whistling. For a moment I thought it was Gran's kettle, but it was coming from next door – the Banerjees' side. I put my ear to the wall. Someone was playing a flute. You could tell it wasn't a record – it was someone playing properly.

"*Gemma!*" Gran shouted from downstairs. "*What you doing up there?*"

By the time I got down the table was laid with bread, ham, cheese and Gran's own pickle. "Need any help?" I asked.

She came through with a pot of tea. "No. Sit."

She sat down and started spreading butter on the bread. I'd never seen Gran so quiet and serious.

"I'm starving," I said.

All you could hear was the clink of her knife against the plate, and she just stared at the table as she ate.

"What happened to Mave then?" I asked.

"Burgled in her own home," she said, still staring. "She answers the front door and there's this boy asking for odd jobs. 'No,' she says, but he keeps

her talking. Then she hears a crash indoors. So she goes back inside and catches some boys red-handed, looking through her cupboards. They got away with her jar of pound coins."

"Terrible," I said.

Gran sighed. "It's getting worse on the Bryn Mawr. We all go down the post office as a mob to get our pensions, frightened something might happen on the way back. This estate is ugly, like it's in the middle of a war. We're all scared on this terrace – scared of opening the door to a stranger. Like prisoners, we are."

She seemed well depressed.

"Heard someone playing the flute next door," I said to change the subject.

"Mr Banerjee's grandson. His family are back in the area."

"Oh yeah?" I said. Not that I was interested – don't have much to do with the Banerjees. "Funny lot, aren't they?" I said.

"No," Gran snapped. "They're lovely people. As far as I'm concerned my own family could take a leaf or two out of their book. They moved back just to be near Mr Banerjee. They look out for each other, and me – more than my own daughter."

"*I'm* here, aren't I?"

"And when was the last time you all came round?"

"Last Sunday."

"No. Sunday before."

"Oh."

We ate in silence.

"I hate cows," I said.

Gran looked up, her forehead crinkled. "What's a cow ever done to you?"

"Something frightening about them," I said. "The way they glare at you." I had her attention, so I told her about what happened with Cowgirl, acting it out big time. "One of the cows was going to trample me to death!"

Gran clucked her tongue.

"Suddenly Cowgirl come from nowhere..."

"Who?"

"Weird girl at school. Cowgirl, we call her. Huge and scary, like her cows. 'Do you no harm,' she says."

"She's right," said Gran.

She was listening and I was glad, even if she must have thought I was a wimp. I told her about Cowgirl's mam cleaning up my cuts at the farm and then watching Cowgirl milk the cows. When I finished Gran said, "What's this girl's name?"

"Kate Thomas."

She nodded. "I think I knew her grandfather."

"How?"

"When I was a land girl during the war. I was scared of cows too, at first. Did my best to avoid them, until I had no choice. Then in no time I realised they're lovely, gentle creatures. I had to milk them – by hand, mind you – none of this machinery business..."

I'd heard her talk before about working on a farm during the war, but I suppose this time I was interested. She was only sixteen. Milking the cows, helping out in the fields and all sorts.

"...I was shattered every night," she said. "Went to bed straight after dinner, sometimes as early as nine o'clock. Then in no time the farmer's wife was knocking at the door again. 'C'mon girls! Up you get.' It never seemed to stop. But after a couple of weeks I got into the stride of it and loved it, like it was in my nature. There was one farm worker I remember – strong, and hardly said a word – a few years older than me he was then. His name was Gareth Thomas. I think he might have been this Kate's granddad."

She was miles away for a few seconds, then she snapped out of it and started stacking the plates. "You need to be getting back to your mam."

"'S'all right," I said, as I preferred staying with Gran after the day I'd had.

"No. You get home, but I want you to invite Kate

here for lunch."

I couldn't believe it. "No way, Gran," I said in a panic.

She banged the plates down and stuck her finger out at me. "I just buried my Ruby, Gemma. Have you forgotten? I don't ask much of you, and if you want that fiver now and again, behind your mam's back, you'll do as I say."

"But I don't know her, Gran!"

"No, that's right – only been to her place for tea, had her mam patch you up and watched her milk cows. Aye, don't know her at all, do you?"

"But..."

"You're scared of her, aren't you?"

"No."

"She's a girl, Gemma, just like you. And you shouldn't call her Cowgirl – her name's Kate. I like the sound of her, so I want you to invite her for lunch, day after tomorrow. You can be here and back to school in no time." I opened my mouth but Gran raised her hand. "You'll invite her and that's that."

Great, I thought. *Totally fab'lous.*

FOUR

"Where you been?" Mam asked.

"Gran's."

"Till now?"

"Mam! What d'you expect me to do? Bury Ruby and go?"

"You been ages, Jamma," said Darren, sprawled out on the settee. "How long's it take to bury a dog?"

"Shut it, you, and don't call me Jamma."

He grinned. "Maybe she was with her boyfriend, Mam?"

"What's this? What boyfriend?"

I felt my face go red, and I haven't even got a

boyfriend. "Ignore him, Mam." Darren was trying to wind me up; always does.

"Did she say she was getting another dog?" Mam asked.

"No. She's just buried Ruby."

"Well, I hope she doesn't."

"Why? What's wrong with her having another dog?"

"Gemma, does it not cross your mind that since your father has been inside, like the plank he is, I need all the help I can get – money-wise and everything else-wise. I don't want your gran throwing her money away on another dog, or cat."

"Why? Cos you want it?"

Mam's eyes became black slits. "What did you say?"

"She said, 'Cos you want it!', Mam," said Darren, leaping to his feet.

"Don't you *ever* give me that lip, Gemma."

"Yeah!" said Darren with a smirk.

That did it. I grabbed him and pushed him back until he crashed against the sideboard. "You shut your nasty, stirring gob."

"Mam!" he called. I banged him against the sideboard again and Dad's statue of Tom Jones rattled. Darren tried to reach my face but my arms are longer.

"Leave him be, Gemma!" Mam shouted, but I didn't.

"I'm fed up of your creeping, your greasy hair, your disgusting pants on the bathroom floor. A rat's cleaner than you…"

"Mam! Get her off."

He pushed me. I pushed him back, and Tom Jones rocked.

"…the way you slurp your cereal, your finger *always* up your nose in front of the TV..." I was making everything Darren's fault – Dad in prison, Mam always having a go, Gran feeling scared to go out.

"That's enough, Gemma!"

Darren snatched at my hair, so I grabbed at his. Mam had her arms round me. "Let him go!" All three of us were wrestling, like we were in a big, angry hug. We crashed into the sideboard. Tom Jones dropped to the floor and smashed. I gave Darren's hair a final, satisfying yank and we all fell down in a pile.

"I've had it with him," I said as I got to my feet.

"She's a nutter!" Darren yelled.

Mam just lay there.

"You all right, Mam?" said Darren. "Shall I call an ambulance?"

"Don't be stupid!" I said.

"Almost killed Mam, you did," said Darren, helping her up.

Mam groaned. "Why are you *always* fighting, eh?"

"It takes two to fight, Mam," I said.

"Doesn't," said Darren, hiding behind her.

"I don't know what's got into you, Gemma, honest to God I don't, but you go to your room now. No supper."

"Had supper at Gran's," I said with a totally-not-bothered look on my face. As I climbed the stairs I heard Darren say, "She's proper mad, isn't she, Mam?"

He's such a creep.

I didn't switch the light on in my bedroom – just lay on the bed and thought about having to ask Cowgirl to Gran's for lunch. But I didn't want to think about it, so I thought of what Dad would be doing in his cell right now. But I didn't want to think about that either. With everything that had happened – not finding the waterfall place, the cows attacking me, Ruby dying on Gran, and me fighting with Mam and Darren – I was suddenly angry, but I didn't want to cry.

I didn't, I didn't, I didn't.

So I smashed the mattress with my fists and screamed as loud as I could.

FIVE

It was freezing on the bus and we were packed together like cows waiting to be milked. Cowgirl was sat at the window staring through a circle she'd wiped on the steamed-up glass. I noticed her hands were red and puffy – maybe that's what happened if you milked cows all the time. I've never seen her smile, not that I go around grinning all day myself.

"Look at her," said Sian, jabbing her chin towards Cowgirl. "How are your cows, girl?" she shouted.

Cowgirl carried on looking out the window.

We all laughed. Sian Jenkins had a nerve. No one messed with her. She thinks it's cool I've got a dad in prison, and she's always asking about him, though I wish she wouldn't. I didn't tell her about meeting Cowgirl an' everything – easier not to.

"OK," said Sian, not letting up. "How are your girls, cow?"

There were more laughs. Cowgirl glanced at me. I could tell what she was thinking – *patched you up and gave you tea, and now you're back on the other side with Sian and the gang.*

We got off the bus, outside school, and Sian waited for her. I could tell she was on one and I didn't like the way it was going. "C'mon Sian!" I said.

"Wait," she said, with her eyes on the bus doors.

Cowgirl was the last to get off.

"I don't like being ignored," Sian said to her.

Cowgirl didn't seem at all scared of her – probably wasn't scared of anyone.

"We'll be late for school," she said.

When she tried to walk on Sian blocked her way and shoved her. Cowgirl hardly moved, like she was a wall.

Just then I spotted Darren with the Tobin brothers.

What's he up to? I thought. The Tobins were well suspect, and hardly ever in school they're excluded so much. Then I heard a yell.

I looked back. Sian was hanging over Cowgirl's

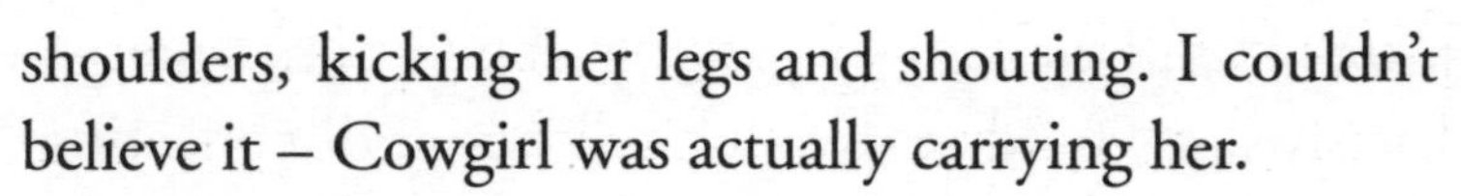

shoulders, kicking her legs and shouting. I couldn't believe it – Cowgirl was actually carrying her.

"Put me down, you cow!"

"Thanks for the compliment!" Cowgirl said as she marched off.

We tried to get her to put Sian down, but Cowgirl just palmed us off like a rugby forward. She's so strong. Sian went on struggling and screaming. Kids were laughing, and I've got to say it *was* funny, but I had to pretend I was angry. Then Cowgirl turned in to the shop by the school.

The shop assistant's face dropped at the sight of her with a girl over her shoulder. "Banana milk, please," Cowgirl asked.

"PUT ME DOWN!" screamed Sian.

"She hates school," Cowgirl said to the assistant as she paid.

Outside, kids had gathered in the street, and as we went along more and more followed us – like a parade, it was. When we entered school we were surrounded. Mr Beale pushed his way through. "What's going on?"

"I was worried we were going to be late for school, sir," said Cowgirl.

"C'mon now, put her down."

As soon as Sian had her feet on the ground she

took a wild swing at Cowgirl, who caught her arm and twisted it. Sian yelled.

"That's enough," said Beale. "Now, what's all this about?"

"She's a cow," said Sian.

"Bit ungrateful, don't you think, sir?" Cowgirl said. "I made sure she didn't miss her first lesson and this is all the thanks I get."

What got me was that most girls would have said Sian did this or said that, but not Cowgirl. It was nothing to her. I've got to say, she was fearless.

During the lunch break I watched her roaming around, like she was on guard duty. She didn't speak to anyone, but I had to make sure Sian didn't see me talking to her. When I saw her go into the loo it was my chance.

There was a girl at the sink inspecting herself in the mirror and two cubicle doors were closed. I went into the third one. I heard a flush go. A girl came out and left with the girl at the sink, so I went for it.

"My gran wants you to come to lunch tomorrow."

There was silence. I banged on the cubicle wall.

"Who's that?"

"Gemma. My gran wants you to come to lunch tomorrow."

"Why?"

"Dunno."

"How does she know me then?"

"I told her about your cows. She used to be a thingy during the war – worked on a farm…"

"Land girl?"

"Yeah, that's it."

I waited. "Well?"

"No thanks."

I heard her pull the flush.

"You got to," I said as she went to wash her hands.

"Why not ask Sian to go?"

"Sian hasn't got cows, has she?" I said. "Look, my gran won't believe I asked you if you don't."

Some girls burst in. I left, feeling really wound up.

When Cowgirl came out I followed her. "You coming or not?"

She turned on me. "Why should I?"

"You both like cows, there's free food and her dog just died."

I glanced behind her and could see Sian and the gang coming towards us.

"Please," I said.

Cowgirl stared at me. "OK. As long as you walk there and back with me."

They were getting closer. "Whatever."

"Does that mean yes?"
Sian was looking right at us.
"School entrance, half-twelve tomorrow."
I was gone.

Six

"What were you doing with the Tobin brothers this morning?" I asked Darren in front of Mam.

He turned white. "Don't know what she's on about, Mam."

The phone call saved him.

"That'll be your dad."

I always let Darren talk to Dad first, partly because he's always up for it but mainly because I never know what to say. I always get nervous waiting to talk to him, like I'm about to go up on stage or read something out in class. So I went to the top of the stairs while Darren was yapping away.

While I sat there I thought of the place with the waterfall – the place I wanted to find. I remembered Dad and Darren daring each other to stick their heads in the icy water to see who could stay under longer. Me and Mam laughing. Darren gave up first. I remember going into a sort of trance as I watched the water falling. It became a blur, like it wasn't real – a magic trick. It just kept pouring down, on and on, forever and ever.

"*Gemma! Come and talk to your dad.*"

My nerves kicked in as I went down the stairs. Darren was back watching TV.

"Where d'you get to?" Mam whispered.

I took the phone off her. "Hi, Dad."

"*Gemma! How's it going?*"

"Fine."

"*School going OK?*"

"Yeah..." I was struggling already. I suppose I could have told him about Cowgirl, but I didn't want to, not in front of Mam, and he wouldn't have been interested anyway.

"What are you doing tonight then?" I said without thinking.

Mam frowned at me. It was a stupid thing to have asked.

"*Oh, me and a couple of the boys are thinking of*

going into town ... a few drinks, you know?" He started laughing.

I didn't like him joking. I would have preferred it if he'd said, "*Stupid thing to say, Gemma! What d'you think I'm doing?*" But that was Dad – always turning everything into a joke. I gave the phone back to Mam as soon as I could and went upstairs.

Later on I heard Mam telling Darren to get off his video game and into bed. When she looked in on me I was already under the duvet and pretending to read.

"Night, Gemma," she said.

"Night, Mam."

She went to close the door.

"Mam?"

"What?"

"D'you remember that picnic?"

"What picnic?"

I felt like saying, *Mam, how often do we go on picnics?*

"Me, you, Dad and Darren. There was a waterfall and a tree. We stayed there all day."

I couldn't see Mam's expression, as the light in the hall made her a shadow in the doorway. "Vaguely," she said. "What about it?"

"Where was it? The place?"

I held my breath.

"I can't remember. Why?"

Because it was a lovely day, I wanted to say. *You were laughing and happy and I want to go back there.*

"Doesn't matter," I said.

Mam stayed at the doorway. I stared at her – the shadow.

"Only a month to go before your dad's out."

"Yeah," I said. Couldn't think of anything else to say. I wanted to ask her what she thought about it. Two years away inside and then he's back just like that, as if he'd been away on a job.

"Night, Gemma."

"Night, Mam."

The shadow closed the door.

Seven

"C'mon, c'mon."

I paced up and down outside the school entrance. Then I saw her strolling along like there was no rush.

"This way," I said.

Cowgirl had a dead-slow walk. Plod, plod, plod. I was happy to lead the way as I didn't want to be seen with her. It was about ten minutes' walk from school to Gran's – two streets and a short cut across the Common – but we didn't have much time.

"You don't want to be doing this, do you?" she asked.

"Whatever."

"We can drop the whole thing if you prefer."

"Look," I said, turning on her. "My gran's dog died, right? I told her about you and your cows cos I thought she might be interested. She asked me to invite you to lunch. You said yes, so here we are. My gran's food's lovely, far better than the stodge at school, so, say, you coming or not? Because we haven't got all day and—"

"All right! All right! Let's go then."

After a bit she said, "What d'you tell her about me?"

"Said you were in my class, you got cows and you live on a farm – 'appy?"

We walked on in silence.

"You must be Gemma's friend Kate?" Gran said, putting her foot straight in it. I didn't say anything, just went through to the lounge. Gran had a lovely spread on the table and the fire was blazing, so to be honest, I didn't care any more. I sat down and started to stuff my face.

It turned out that Gran did know Cowgirl's granddad, so they talked and talked. Cowgirl was different – smiley and bright. Gran was going on about being a land girl, the early starts and milking by hand and everything.

"How many cows have you got?" Gran asked her.

"Twelve," said Cowgirl. "We used to have more before the foot-an'-mouth came along."

She suddenly looked sad.

"Oh, that was awful," said Gran. "Killing all those cows and burning them. Such a waste."

"What?" I said. "Killing and burning?"

They both looked at me. "Oh Gemma, don't you remember? Cows piled up like wood on a bonfire. You could see the smoke from here, and the smell – terrible, it was."

"Oh yeah," I said, lying.

"The farmers got compensation though, didn't they?" Gran asked.

Cowgirl stared at her plate. "Yes," she said. "But it wasn't the same. While we waited for the compensation Mam got herself a part-time job in town. Then when the money did come, Dad bought a smaller herd and set himself up as a landscape gardener, which is what he's always wanted. As he got more and more work I took over the milking."

"You do it all?" Gran asked.

Cowgirl shrugged. "I like it."

Gran was smiling at her. "Well, I think you've got it just about right, Kate. How many girls up and down the country could say they were doing as much? I think you're a star."

Cowgirl took a bite out of her sandwich, as if she hadn't heard. "Glad I don't have to milk them all by hand though – take me hours."

"I used to talk to them while I milked them," said Gran. "Even sing them a song sometimes. They're such lovely, gentle creatures. Can't understand why anyone would be frightened of them." They both glanced at me, just as I pushed the last part of a fruit bun into my mouth.

"Reckon you could still remember how to milk a cow, Mrs Matthews?" Cowgirl asked.

"I don't see why not. Yes, yes, I think I could."

"Well, why not come up to the farm and give it a go?"

Gran's face lit up. "Really?"

Cowgirl nodded.

"I'd love to."

I panicked. "You can't," I said with my mouth full.

"Why ever not?" asked Gran.

"How would you get up there?"

"Oh, my own granddaughter," she said. "If you had your way I'd be locked up in a care home. Roger or Mr Banerjee could give me a lift." She turned to Cowgirl. "They're neighbours of mine. Would you

mind an extra person?"

"No, that'll be OK, Mrs Matthews."

"Please call me Lilly," says Gran.

So that was that. But the thing that got to me, apart from the fact that I had to walk back to school with Cowgirl, was that Gran had called her a "star" and I couldn't remember the last time anyone called me a star, if ever.

EIGHT

We went out the back way and into the alley that runs behind the terrace. As we were saying goodbye to Gran there was a shout from next door. "Lilly! Lilly! Got them this time!"

"Roger?" called Gran.

Gran's neighbour, Roger, came into the alley from his backyard holding on to Jamie and his mate, Ryan, who were struggling and swiping out at him. Ryan is Sian's brother, which made me a bit nervy.

"Little brats!" said Roger. "They tried it again, Lil. You know, like with Mave, one round the front ringing the doorbell. Well, I smelled a rat, didn't I?

Found this pair in my lounge, rifling around. Do us a favour and call the police, I got my hands full."

"Oh, this place has gone rotten," said Gran.

"We did nothing!" shouted Jamie.

"Zero to nick anyway," said Ryan.

"What's going on, Lilly?" a woman called down from a house nearby.

"Roger caught a couple of boys in his house, Polly."

"Oh, that's twice this week," the woman at the window said. "And poor Mave at number ten is only just getting over it!"

Ryan kicked out and caught Roger on the shin. He yelped and let go of them. They made a dash for it but ran straight into Cowgirl. She grabbed them like they were a couple of shopping bags and cracked their heads together. Smack. They yelped.

"That's Sian's brother," I said, nodding at Ryan.

He looked up at Cowgirl. "And she'll kill you when I tell her!"

"That supposed to make me let you go, is it?"

She was so cool about it, but I was worried.

Mr Banerjee and Polly came out into the back alley.

"Get her off, Gemma!" Jamie said to me.

"Go on. Let 'em go," I said.

Gran and Roger turned on me. "What? NO!"

"It's all right, is it, Gemma?" said Gran. "These

boys – and girls too – making our lives along this terrace a misery? The Bryn Mawr estate was a lovely place years ago when they first built it. My back door was always open, to all and sundry…"

"That's right," said Roger.

"A community," added Mr Banerjee.

"Aye. Those days are well gone now," said Gran. "The doors are double bolted, and we don't go out after dark. It's horrible, Gemma, and it makes me glad to be at the end of my life rather than at the beginning."

They were all looking at me as if I'd been the one who'd broken into Roger's house. Then I spotted Darren coming along the alley.

"That's the monkey that rang my doorbell!" said Roger, pointing at him.

"Darren!" Gran and me shouted at the same time. "Come 'ere!"

"They made me do it, Gran," he said, pointing at Ryan and Jamie.

I grabbed him. "You wait till I tell Mam!"

"Oh I see, Gemma," said Gran. "Changed your tune now it's your own brother that's involved."

I couldn't win.

"He's my neighbour, Darren!" said Gran. "Not that it makes it right if he wasn't. What d'you think they

were doing round the back while you rang the bell?"

"It was just a laugh."

"My own flesh and blood," said Gran.

"Would you hold on to this one?" Cowgirl said to Roger, handing Jamie over to him. She slung Ryan over her shoulder, as if he was nothing more than a jacket.

"NO! Put me down!" he shouted.

Cowgirl turned to Roger. "I think I can manage that one too." Roger lifted up Jamie so she had one on each shoulder, struggling away.

"Thanks for the lunch, Lilly," she said.

"Pleasure's all mine," said Gran.

"See you up at the farm," Cowgirl said as she walked off with Ryan and Jamie hanging down her back.

Gran watched her go with a big grin on her face. "You got a special friend there, Gemma," she said. "You can learn a lot from her instead of that ne'er-do-well Sian. And you," she said to Darren. "I'll be speaking to your mam, make no mistake."

So off we went, and I'm thinking I've got to walk back into school with Cowgirl, who happens to have two boys slung over her shoulders, one of them being Sian Jenkins's brother – 'appy days.

NINE

We went back across the scuzzy Mawr Common, towards school. It was bad enough to have to walk back with Cowgirl, without the extra attention we were getting. She had her arms wrapped around both boys' legs like she was carrying two sacks of fodder to the milking shed. Ryan started hitting Cowgirl as he hung over her shoulder. She stopped. "See those stingy nettles?" she said. "You hit me one more time and I'll walk through them, backwards."

"I feel sick," said Jamie.

"Teach you to bother people who do no harm."

Ryan hit her again. "PUT US DOWN!"

"Right, that's it!" Cowgirl went up to the nettle bushes, turned and walked into them backwards. Ryan and Jamie screamed like they were on a roller coaster.

Kids followed us as if it was a daily event, and so by the time we got to the school entrance there was a crowd. Then Sian was standing in front of us. God, she looked angry. "Put my brother down!"

"Not yet. Almost there."

Sian turned on me and my knees went wobbly. "Why didn't you stop her?"

"She was with her, Sian," said Ryan, upside down. "She was there."

I pointed at Darren. "I was sorting *my* brother out, wasn't I?"

"She and Cowgirl were round my gran's!" said Darren, the grass.

"Cosy," said Sian, glaring at me, and I knew that was it – I was in deep. She turned to Cowgirl. "Put 'em down – now!"

"No."

Sian grabbed her brother and started to tug. Karen, one of Sian's best mates, held Jamie, but Cowgirl carried on walking as if she was a horse pulling a plough. Ryan and Jamie screamed. Everyone was laughing, and then Cowgirl let go. Ryan, Jamie, Sian and Karen ended up in a pile on the ground. I would have laughed too, if I hadn't been thinking about what Sian was going to do to me.

TEN

"I didn't know what they were doing, Mam. Honest."

"You were naughty, Darren," she said, staring at the TV, having a smoke.

"Is that all you're going to say?" I shouted. "He was ringing the doorbell so that his mates could break in the back to help themselves – burglars!"

"Don't shout, Gemma! I don't come home to listen to you shouting, all right?"

"Yeah, Jamma," said Darren. "Mam's watching TV and having a rest. You can see that," he added as he slid on to the settee, like a creep. "I wasn't robbing, Mam. Honest to God."

"They were going to call the police!" I said.

"Who were?"

"Gran and Roger."

"Oh, I've never liked that Roger – rude, he is, and miserable!"

Darren leaned his head on Mam's arm. "Cowgirl dragged them through stingy nettles, Mam."

"Who is this girl?"

"Kate Thomas," I said, folding my arms. I was stood in the middle of the lounge like I was the mam and they were the kids.

"Massive, she is," said Darren.

"What was she doing round your gran's, anyway?"

"Robbing her, for all we know," said Darren.

"Gran invited her," I said, though I was past caring. "She lives on a farm, milking cows."

"Should have seen their faces after going through the stingies, Mam – all lumpy they were."

"Oh! I knew it was box fourteen!" said Mam, staring at the TV. "Seventy-five grand she lost! Should have listened to me."

"She should have listened to you, Mam," said Darren.

I couldn't bear watching him crawl, so I went up to my room.

❀❀❀

I took out a jewellery box Gran had given me years ago, not that I've got any proper jewellery, and I looked at the dried grass and leaves inside.

When we went for that picnic, me and Darren went exploring – we used to get on OK then. I was wearing lovely new sandals Dad had bought me, and they'd got all dirty. It was a few days later that the police arrived and arrested him. Mam was crying. I was crying. It was horrible. Dad said he'd be back, but he wasn't. He got sent to prison for petty larceny and fraud, which is a posh way of saying stealing and cheating.

Well, the day after he was arrested I was putting on my new shoes and I noticed dried grass still stuck to the soles. I cried. Not because they were new and all dirty, but because when the leaves and grass got stuck to the shoes everything was OK. Then a few days later it was all not OK.

I don't know why I did it, but I pulled off all the bits of dried stuff and put them in the jewellery box. Silly, I suppose – just dirt, people'd say. No one knows what it is, 'cept me, and all from a place I remember but can't find.

I wondered if Dad ever thought about that picnic at the waterfall. He had no worries sitting in his cell, not like me. I had to go back to school and face Sian, and it was all Cowgirl's fault.

"Why did I have to open my big mouth and tell Gran?" I said out loud.

I closed the box and fell back on my bed.

ELEVEN

The great thing about cycling is that it's good for you, but no one thinks you're doing proper exercise. See, if I'd started jogging around the Bryn Mawr everyone would've made fun of me, but being on your bike lots goes unnoticed. And when you cycle you leave everything behind, like my brother Darren, or facing Sian at school.

It was a cold day, but lovely and sunny too. So I cycled up to the farm. It would only take me about twenty minutes to get there, but I wanted to go the long way, from the top of the valley and down the hill – eyes wide open this time. I loved the wind and the speed. Fantastic. I thought I was going to take off.

There was no sign of anyone when I got there. A truck was parked outside the farmhouse with "Nigel Thomas Landscape Gardener" written on the side.

"Looking for Kate?"

I turned. There was a man standing there. He was big and stocky, with curly black and grey hair – the man who had stopped when I was lying in the road. It was Cowgirl's dad. I could tell because he had the same narrow, serious eyes.

"Yes," I said.

"She's in there." He nodded towards the milking shed. "I remember you," he said. "Lying in the road. Came up here, didn't you? My wife said you fell over."

I nodded.

"Not going to sue us, are you?"

I couldn't tell if he was joking or not.

"Wouldn't have imagined Kate had any friends," he muttered as he walked past me and into the house.

I decided I didn't like him.

I wheeled my bike to the milking shed and leaned it against the wall. Someone was singing inside. I peered round the doorpost and there was Cowgirl hosing down the floor. I watched her for a while. She seemed happy, scrubbing the floor and singing away – something in Welsh. When she saw me her expression turned from happy to annoyed. "Shouldn't creep up on people!"

"Sorry," I said.

"Lilly here?"

"No. I came on my bike."

"Well, you'll have to wait."

Making people feel welcome seemed to run in the family, I thought. I stood there, like a cow waiting my turn for milking, while she carried on hosing and sweeping the water out. Thorough job she made of it, I've got to say.

Finally, she turned off the water. "I'll go and get Jane."

"That your mam?"

"What? No, she's a cow."

"Who? Your mam?"

"NO! Jane. Jane is a cow, you stupid—"

"You invited my gran, you did," I snapped. "You didn't invite me, but she's my gran and … and I want her to have a nice day…" My voice went thin. Cowgirl leaned her brush against the wall.

"I'll get Jane. You wait here for your gran."

She went off and I sat on the step of the shed, wishing I'd just carried on cycling along the top of the valley. It wasn't long before I heard Roger's car straining to get up the hill. By the time it turned into the farm it was sounding like it was about to explode. Roger stopped the car next to the shed and got out. "It better still be on," he said. "Didn't think she'd make it coming up from the Mawr!"

Gran sat there waiting, so I opened the door for her, like a chauffeur.

"He's been moaning from the moment we left," she mumbled. "Everything all right?"

"Yeah." Then I saw Mr Banerjee getting out the back. "What's he doing here?" I whispered.

Gran frowned and came close to me. "Gemma, do me a favour, I been looking forward to today so don't show us up. He's come to see the cow, like me. And as a Hindu he has more right to be here than us." She turned to him. "Isn't that right, Mr Banerjee? The cow is a special animal in India?"

He nodded and smiled. "Very special."

Mr Thomas came towards us.

"Like Cardiff central station here today," he said. "You all come to see Kate?"

"Yes," said Gran. "She invited me up. I'm Lilly, Gemma's grandmother. Kind of her to invite me. See, during the war I used to be—"

"Didn't know she was giving guided tours," he said. "Make sure you sterilise your shoes before you

make contact with any of the cows. We don't want you bringing your Bryn Mawr germs up here."

"Of course," said Gran. "If it's not convenient…"

Mr Thomas nodded at something behind us. "Here she is."

We turned and there was Cowgirl leading a cow towards us. Her dad walked up to her. I couldn't hear what he said, but Cowgirl went red and said something back.

"I don't care," I heard him say. She walked past him like he wasn't there, and the cow followed.

"They get foot-an'-mouth, it'll be your fault," her dad called.

Cowgirl ignored him and brought the cow over to Gran. "Lilly, I'd like you to meet Jane."

"Hello, my lovely," Gran said as she stroked the cow's head. "Oh Kate, I hope we haven't got you in trouble?"

"No, Lilly. We'll just make sure you've got proper footwear and clean hands, like I was going to do anyway. Jane's the best behaved of the herd. She'll let you milk her the old-fashioned way."

Mr Thomas started his truck and drove out of the yard. Cowgirl watched him go. "First things first," she said. "We need to get you all in wellies and your hands washed."

She was like a different girl. Her dad had joked about her giving a tour, but that was what it was like. She soon sorted us out with wellies. "These should fit you, Gemma," she said, which was the first time I'd ever heard her use my name. She got us washing our hands, supervising us like a teacher. Then she led us back to the milking shed where the cow was waiting for us.

"Here you are, Lilly," said Cowgirl, as she placed a bucket and a stool under the cow. I was nervous for Gran, because she did go on about her time on the farm during the war and here she was being tested, sort of.

"It's been many years, Jane," she said. "I'll do my best."

The cow glanced at Gran as if she understood.

Gran bent down and took a thingy in each hand – teats, she said they were called – and began to squeeze them. Nothing happened at first. I glanced at Cowgirl watching her, then there was the sound of something drilling into the bucket. It was amazing how much milk came out with each squeeze.

"Natural, you are," said Cowgirl, but Gran just carried on like she had a job to do. The cow kept eating the fodder and the bucket was half full of milk before long. I've got to say I felt proud of Gran.

She finally stopped and sat back with a groan. She grinned. "Ooh, I'd forgotten what a strain it was, bending over for long." She looked up at me. "Going to have a go, Gemma?"

I wasn't expecting that. "Nah," I said. "Not bothered."

"Oh, go on," Gran said. "It's not many times in life you get the chance to do something like this."

My cheeks became all hot. I shook my head. "No thanks."

"I would like to try, please," said Mr Banerjee.

So he had a go too.

Twelve

We took Jane back to the field to rejoin the rest of the herd, and we stayed at the gate watching them for a while. Some were lying down, and others chewed at the grass.

"Granddad told me we had over two hundred head of cattle before I was born," Cowgirl said. "We had about fifty before the foot-an'-mouth outbreak, and now twelve." She pointed across the field. "These fields were all ours. Sold to Mostyn's farm now."

"Old miser Mostyn," said Roger.

"But if it's Mostyn's field," said Gran, "how come you're still using it?"

"We rent it off him, for the cows to graze on."

"Aren't there any baby cows?" I asked.

"No," she said. "They're away now."

"Why?"

"Ever wondered how it is that cows give milk all year round?" Gran asked me. The way they were looking at me I got the feeling they knew something I didn't.

"Their calves are taken from them and we take their milk because they carry on producing it."

It sounded cruel. "But the calves are their … babies."

"But you want your milk from the supermarket like everyone else, don't you?"

"In India, we share the milk with the calves," said Mr Banerjee.

"And you'd never kill the cow. Isn't that right?" asked Gran.

Mr Banerjee shook his head and smiled. "Never."

We watched the cows in the field for a while longer, and then headed back to the farmhouse. Cowgirl's mam came out to meet us.

"Hello, Gemma," she said. "How's your leg?"

"Fine, thanks."

She was introduced to Gran, Mr Banerjee and Roger – Kerry, her name was – and she invited us into the kitchen for tea. The cheery, chatty Cowgirl was gone as she silently helped her mam. Gran went on about what a lovely day she was having.

"It must be hard for farmers these days," said Mr Banerjee.

Kerry nodded. "When I married my husband this was a busy working farm and we made a good living. Now farmers are either the big timers like Don Mostyn or else you're struggling and looking how you can make ends meet. The days are numbered for that herd."

Cowgirl's lips went tight.

"You're selling them?" asked Gran.

"Not one of Kate's favourite topics," said Kerry, "but we've not much choice. They're past their prime now, and Mostyn wants that field back."

"They've got lots to give yet," said Cowgirl, like she was talking to herself.

"How old are they?" I asked.

"Some are six, some seven."

"Six! Is that all? How long would they live for if..."

"Twenty, thirty years," Mr Banerjee replied.

Cowgirl nodded, then a truck pulled up outside and I saw her glance at her mam. The door of the truck slammed and in walked her dad. He looked down at us.

"You know, Kerry, I think Kate's hit on a good sideline here," he said. "Farm tours with tea and cake thrown in. What d'you reckon?"

Kerry laughed. "Well, you never know."

"I'd pay," said Gran with a smile. "You must be very proud of Kate."

"Takes after her granddad, she does," Mr Thomas said.

"Yes, I remember Gareth well," said Gran. "He didn't say a lot, but I liked him. And I've never seen anyone in my life work harder than your father."

Gran had picked her moment. Mr Thomas's stern look vanished. He seemed sort of itchy, like he wished he hadn't come in. "Maybe it was because the world was at war," Gran continued, "but he was up before anyone else and in bed after everyone else, seven days a week. Then he was called up and I remember he was in the papers when he returned – got a medal for valour."

"That's right," said Kerry. She walked over to the wall and lifted off a picture. "There he is. That's Nigel in his mam's arms."

Gran took the photo and smiled. "This must be, what? Twenty, thirty years after I knew him. But he's the same. A giant."

I looked at the faded black and white picture.

He did look like a giant – he was huge, with broad shoulders, and there were Cowgirl's narrow eyes.

"I'm sorry to hear things aren't exactly rosy for you these days," said Gran.

Mr Thomas's face switched back to angry. He glared at Cowgirl. "Why don't you just tell everything to the local rag?"

"All I said was—"

"All you said was too much!"

She was embarrassed and I felt sorry for her. Gran laid the picture on the table. "I didn't mean to cause offence, Mr Thomas." She stood up, scraping back her chair. "We should go."

"Right you are," said Roger, getting up.

Gran put her hand on Cowgirl's arm. "You're from a proud line, Kate. Don't forget it. I can't thank you enough, and you're always welcome to come for lunch at my home, with your mam's permission, of course."

Kerry smiled. "Well, Kate had nothing but good things to say about you. Thank you, Lilly, and you, Gemma."

Mr Banerjee helped Gran on with her coat. She didn't look at Mr Thomas until she had buttoned it up, then she said, "I wish you and this farm well, whatever you choose to do."

I was still standing there as they walked out. "I'll see you in school, Kate." She glanced up from the picture. I smiled and she nodded.

I walked outside just as Roger's car started up with a bang. Gran waved at me and I watched them drive away. The noise from his car faded as I wheeled my bike past the farmhouse. I expected to hear an argument, but I couldn't hear a thing, as if no one was home. I started cycling and thought about Kate. I felt different about her, even though she was mostly rude to me.

I was going maximum speed downhill when I remembered Sian and screamed at the wind.

THIRTEEN

"So?" Sian was right in my face. "How come you were just standing by while Cowgirl picked on my brother?"

I wondered why she had it in for Kate. I wanted to be cool and calm, and not feel my legs trembling. Tracy, Karen and Jo were smirking at me over her shoulder, glad that someone else was in deep – I knew that feeling.

"My gran invited her round, all right?"

"No, it's not all right," she said. "You and Cowgirl mates now, or what?"

My heart thumped. I knew if I said "yes" Sian

would single me out and I'd be the one on the bus by the window. I'd be the one on my own.

I felt bad saying, "No."

I was first out at lunchtime and glad I'd brought my bike. I just wanted to get away. On the way to Gran's I imagined winning the Tour de France – first woman ever. I went in the backyard, parked my bike and knocked on the back door.

Gran opened up. "Oh, Gemma."

She looked surprised. I went in and noticed she had the table laid with two plates. "Expecting someone?"

"As a matter of fact I am," she said, going back into the kitchen.

I guessed it must be grumpy Roger, but if Gran was getting company, 'specially with Ruby gone, why should I care? She came back from the kitchen with an extra plate.

"Sorry Gran," I said, "but I needed to get away from school."

"It's OK. I invited Kate. Something I wanted to ask her."

The doorbell went. "That'll be her."

"Kate?"

"Yes. Let her in, would you?"

I wondered if I'd missed something.

"All right?" said Kate as I opened the door.

"Hello, Kate," said Gran behind me. "Come into the warm and sit yourself down."

I'd gone to Gran's to get away from school only to find she was expecting Kate without telling me.

"I'll get off, Gran," I said.

"Oh, nonsense. Sit yourself down."

"Not hungry. I was just stopping by on my way home."

I went out the back.

"Gemma?"

"Got to dash, Gran," I shouted as I closed the door.

Standing in the backyard I could feel my eyes go watery. I went to get my bike and gasped.

It was gone.

I ran out into the lane. At the far end I could see a boy riding it away.

"Oi!" I screamed.

I ran full pelt, but no matter how much cycling you do it doesn't automatically make you a good runner. I got about halfway down the alley before I had to stop, out of breath. He was well gone.

"Aw, what's the matter, Gemma?"

It was Ryan with a group of boys.

"Who was it?" I asked. "Who took it?"

He smirked. "Took what?"

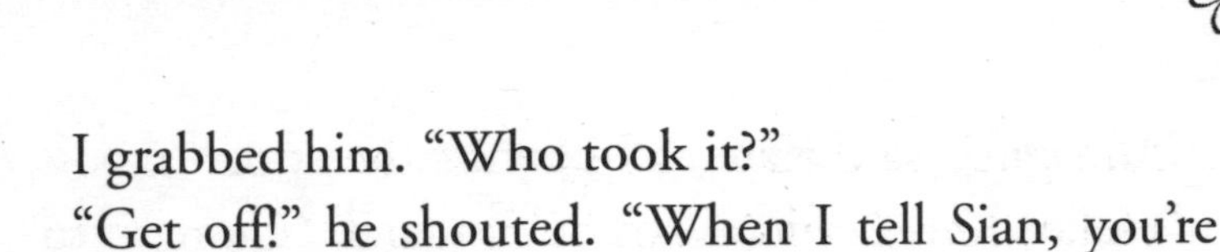

I grabbed him. "Who took it?"

"Get off!" he shouted. "When I tell Sian, you're dead."

"Who was it?"

He kicked me, and before I knew it, the other boys joined in. I was no match for them. One was pulling my jumper, and another was karate-chopping my arm to make me let go, and all the while I shook Ryan until he became a blur.

"Hey!"

Someone was pulling them off me.

I turned to see this boy – tall with olive skin and jet-black hair – gorgeous, he was. I'd never seen him before.

"Boys attacking a girl," he said.

"What's it to you?" Ryan said.

"Do your mothers know you do this?"

"Jog on."

The gorgeous boy pulled something from his rucksack. I saw a flash of silver, like a sword. The boys stepped back. He laughed. "Scared of music?" he said, holding a flute.

"Weirdo," said Ryan.

The gorgeous boy started to play and walked towards them. They backed away, as if his playing had magic powers. They shouted nasty things at him, but he just carried on playing. After they'd gone he turned to me. I must have looked a mess – hair hanging over my face and my jumper all out of shape.

"What was all that about?" he asked.

"Someone stole my bike and they saw who it was."

I felt like crying but it was the last thing I wanted to do in front of him. He seemed so concerned for me.

"Your gran's my grandfather's neighbour, isn't she?"

I nodded.

"We should call the police."

It was nice that he said "we", but I shook my head. "No point. It's gone now."

Just saying that opened the floodgates and I started to cry.

I turned and ran.

"Hey!"

My lovely bike was gone, and I'd cried in front of a gorgeous boy.

FOURTEEN

I'd never bunked off in my life, but I couldn't face going back to school. So I went home and had a bath. I lay there feeling sorry for myself. I thought about Mr Banerjee's grandson. He must have been the flute player I'd heard through the wall at Gran's. I wondered what his name was. Amazing eyes, he had, and lovely teeth and hair. I felt ashamed, since I was never exactly friendly to his granddad. I decided I'd make more of an effort. Then I remembered my bike and sank under the water, making my groan turn into bubbles.

After the bath I made four slices of jam on toast

and watched TV lying on the settee. It was lovely, though I felt a bit nervous knowing I should be in school. I fell asleep and woke when I heard the key in the lock. Mam walked in.

"What you doing here?"

"Felt sick, Mam. Went in this morning. Wasn't feeling well so I went to Gran's at lunchtime. Then someone nicked my bike."

"Oh, Gemma. D'you lock it?"

"No, Mam. It was in Gran's backyard."

"Well, what d'you expect on the Mawr estate? Might as well put a note on it saying 'free bike'. And don't ask me for a new one cos it isn't going to happen, not unless we win the lottery."

I was stupid not to lock my bike and stupid to expect any sympathy. Then Darren came in and said, "Sian's after you – said you beat up her brother. You're dead."

"What's this?" asked Mam.

"I didn't beat up anyone. They set on me – four of them. They saw who took my bike, Mam. They saw!"

"And you expect them to tell you who it was, just like that, do you? It's the Bryn Mawr. You're not going to change it."

"So I do nothing, do I?"

"Look, I know you liked that bike, Gemma, but you'll just have to notch it up to experience."

"No, Mam, I'm going to the police."

"Oh, brilliant. The daughter of Robbie Matthews turns up and asks for her bike back. Know what the police'll say? They'll say what goes around comes around. I'm sorry, Gemma, but you might as well start saving for a new one."

I was determined not to cry.

"Yeah," said Darren. "And I'll tell the hospital to expect you after Sian's done with you."

Mam turned on him before I had the chance. "And you can shut up. I want peace when I come home. D'you understand?"

Darren went all meek. "Yes, Mam." Then he grinned at me, but I didn't care. I had bigger things to worry about, like who nicked my bike and surviving the showdown with Sian.

FIFTEEN

I was packed into the aisle of the bus and scared stiff. When we got to Sian's stop, there she was with Tracy and the rest. The adrenaline started pumping round my body. She was looking for me as soon as she got on. There's something hard and cruel about Sian's eyes, like she's hunting – out for the kill.

"You and me gonna talk," she called out when she saw me. There were too many kids in the aisle for her to get to me, so as the bus went along I looked out of the window. I imagined myself cycling in a road race at the Olympics, leading the pack with my legs going like pistons. Then I realised the bus

had stopped, and the adrenaline started up again as everyone began to get off.

Sian came straight up to me. She looked like a dog baring its teeth.

"Why d'you hit Ryan?"

"I didn't—"

There was a gasp when she slapped me. All the usual chattering stopped. My cheek stung, and I felt a tear run down from my eye. Kids were all around us, like they'd been told to make a neat circle.

"I didn't hit him." My voice was shaking.

"Standing in the alley minding his own business, he was," she said. "Then you turn up and have a go."

I braced myself for another slap when Kate pushed her way into the circle.

"Hello."

"You keep out of this," Sian said as she stabbed a finger towards her. "This your bodyguard?" she said to me.

I didn't feel so scared with Kate stood there. "I didn't hit your brother," I said again. "My bike got nicked and he saw who took it."

"He said he didn't see nothing and you were asking him to grass."

"If he didn't see nothing he couldn't grass then, could he?"

That was it. I could tell, just by the look in her eyes, that I was out of the gang. Part of me was relieved. She turned and walked off. Karen, Tracy and Jo sneered at me before following her. The circle of kids broke up, disappointed.

Kate and me made our way into school.

"Heard your bike got stolen," she said. "Is that why you weren't around in the afternoon?"

I nodded.

"Your gran was worried she'd upset you."

"Nah," I lied.

"She asked me to tell you to go round hers today, for lunch."

"You going?" I asked.

"Unless it's a problem?"

I shrugged.

I didn't see Sian as we left at lunchtime, and we made straight for the terrace.

"Any news?" Gran asked as soon as she opened the door.

"About what?"

"Your bicycle, of course. Oh, why didn't you lock it, Gemma?"

"Gran, don't *you* start. It got nicked, all right? My fault. Not blaming anyone except me, stupid me!" I

started crying. "I loved that bike…"

"Come 'ere." Gran hugged me, which set me off all the more.

Up in Gran's bathroom I washed my face. My eyes were puffy, and my cheek was still red from Sian's slap. I listened at the wall but couldn't hear anything from next door, so I guessed "gorgeous Banerjee" was at school – probably some posh one for boys and girls that play the flute or the piano.

On the landing I could hear Kate and Gran talking. I made my way down, feeling a bit embarrassed. I went in and saw a twenty-pound note by my plate.

"What's this?"

"Towards your new bike," said Gran. She raised her hand. "Not a word, Gemma. You loved that bike – it's helped you get healthy. You're too thin, mind you, but I'd rather have that than a granddaughter that has to be rolled down the road. Put it away and before you know it you'll be back on your bike." She chuckled. " 'On your bike!' Witty of me."

"Thanks, Gran."

As we started eating I wanted to ask about Mr Banerjee's grandson, as casually as I could.

"I heard a flute playing next door again."

A total lie but I was desperate.

"Oh, that's Mr Banerjee's grandson," said Gran.

"Lovely young man. Studying the flute, he is, at that academy in Cardiff. Very concerned, he was, about you and your bike, Gemma."

I nodded. "What's his..." *Keep cool,* I thought. "What's his name?"

"Karuna."

"Karuna," I repeated.

Gran and Kate were staring at me like they'd sussed I fancied him. I just knew my cheeks were glowing.

"Lovely food, Gran," I said, to change the subject. She looked a bit surprised.

Kate and her got talking and I was just happy to listen.

"Mostyn's putting pressure on Dad for the money he owes him, and he wants his field back, where the cows graze. Mostyn's got loads of cows – he doesn't need ours."

"Oh, it all seems such a shame," said Gran. "I remember when your granddad, Gareth, used to bring the cows down to graze on the Common. That was before they built the Bryn Mawr around it, of course."

"He had Commoners' Rights, Lilly," said Kate.

"What's that?" I asked.

"Granddad was allowed to take the cows down to the Mawr Common to graze for free."

"And the grass was cut back by the cows in return," said Gran. "Animal mowers. I loved seeing them there. Things were so simple back then. I know that sounds like old fuddy-duddy talk, but they were. I can't for the life of me see why there's trouble all the time – violence and noise and cruelty. Polly Williams had a window smashed the other day for no reason. It's just sheer nastiness. I just don't know where it comes from."

I suppose I'd never really thought about it before, but all you hear on the news is stabbings or killing and murder – like Gran said, nastiness everywhere.

Afterwards, Kate and me walked along the alley back to school. We didn't talk much, though I didn't feel uncomfortable this time.

"What did he look like – the boy that took your bike?"

"He was too far off. But even if I knew he's not about to tell where it is."

"Red, isn't it?"

I nodded. "It's a hybrid. I'd like a proper racer, but the roads round here would shake me to bits."

"What was it called – the make, I mean?"

"Vortex. Why?"

Kate shrugged. "Keep an eye out for it."

"Thanks." Apart from Gran it was the first nice

thing anyone had said to me in ages. As we neared the end of the alley I noticed a group of boys gathered around one of the back doors. "Here we go," I mumbled.

"Nutter!" one of them shouted into a backyard.

"God, he stinks!" another boy said.

"Go'way!" I heard someone shout back. It was where "mad Morris" lived.

Kate walked right up to them.

"Yeah, wha'?" a boy said. Then his eyes flashed wide. "Cowgirl?"

Kate nodded. "That's right. Wanna lift to school?"

The boys backed away. "Freako!" they called.

Kate ignored them and knocked on the door.

"What you doing?" I asked her.

"Go'way!" I heard Morris shout.

"You all right?" Kate asked through the door.

Suddenly it jerked open and Morris stood there in his stained clothes, looking like a proper tramp. "Go'way!"

"Just checking you're all right," said Kate.

Morris slammed the door shut.

"That's Morris," I whispered. "He's a proper mental case."

Kate walked on. The door opened again and Morris was staring at me in his green cardy, stretched out like he was wearing an old dress. I caught a whiff of him before he slammed the door shut again.

"God, he does stink," I said, catching up with Kate.

"Well, he *must* be mental then," she said.

I knew she was being sarky. She made me feel guilty, 'specially after what Gran had said about the way things were on the estate. "He does no harm, I suppose."

As we walked I noticed the rubbish on the ground. It was like I'd never seen it before – broken furniture left on the pavement, smashed TVs and graffiti everywhere. It was ugly.

I kept my head down that afternoon at school. Didn't even look across at Sian, but just before last period we were going into the corridor and she came up to me.

"Had a word with Ryan about your bike. Said he didn't see who took it and I believe him. But tell you what he did say – said your brother Darren was with 'em in the alley. And when you came out shouting for your bike, Ryan reckons your brother vanished. Odd, isn't it? Maybe you should be looking closer to home before you go pointing fingers." She grinned the nastiness grin. "We're not done, Cowgirl Two, not by a long way."

❀❀❀

That night I went into Darren's room. The fiver I held up in the air caught his attention and stopped him calling out. He paused the video game he was playing – the usual shooting, bombing and killing.

"What's that?" he asked, like he was hypnotised.

"A fiver, isn't it."

"What's it for?"

"It's for you." He went to take it. "Steady, Darren. I want information."

"I don't know who took your bike, all right?"

"Well, you could ask round, couldn't you?"

"Cost you more than a fiver."

"Sian told me."

"Told you what?"

"You were there."

"Was not!"

"Oh yeah? Your mate Ryan's a grass for nothing, is he?"

"I saw nothing!"

"Well, first you weren't there, now you saw nothing? Which is it, Darren? Did you tip someone off and take a slice of the money they got for the bike?"

"I've done nothing. Telling Mam."

He went for the door. I grabbed him and covered his mouth. His eyes widened. "You can tell Mam

what you like but I know you were there, and I won't forget it, Darren. My bike. Your own sister's bike. Nasty. Nasty."

I left him to stew.

SIXTEEN

It was pouring with rain Saturday morning, but Mam needed me to go to the supermarket. "Here's the list," she said. "And your gran called – I said you'd pick her up a few things too."

I nodded. Mam looked at me, then shouted upstairs, "Darren! Go with your sister to the shops."

"*Aw, Mam!*" he called from his room.

"It's OK," I said. "No point two of us getting wet."

To be honest I wanted to get out. I couldn't stop thinking about my bike, and I couldn't get away without it, not properly away. So I was walking in the rain; not that cycling in the rain is fun but at least

you get there quicker. The supermarket was busy, but I was too fed up to rush, so I took my time. I smelled Morris before I saw him. He was holding a can of something an inch from his eyes. *I'll make an effort*, I thought.

"Hello, Morris."

"Go'way!" he snapped.

"Sorry." Least I tried.

As I walked away I heard, "Chopped or peeled?"

He was holding out a tin of tomatoes towards me. I went back and read the label. "Chopped," I said.

"I need *peeled* tomatoes not chopped!" he shouted. People glanced over. I could feel my embarrassment making me go hot, so I found the right tin. "Peeled plum tomatoes," I said as I handed it to him. He took it and placed it in his basket. "Cooking breakfast, I was. Emptied the can into the saucepan – they were chopped. Ruined that breakfast."

"Terrible," I said.

"Now I need tinned corned beef. Tinned, mind you."

What could I do? I walked down the aisle. Morris and his smell were right behind me. "Here you are," I said. "Tinned corned beef. Two varieties."

"Co-op own brand."

I handed it to him.

"Potato and leek soup – tin."

And so I became Morris's helper that morning.

As we went along the shop assistants would glance at me in sympathy. At one point a bloke went past and said, "Morris, do yourself a favour – have a bath, man."

It was so rude. "Don't smell like a bunch o' roses yourself!" I said back.

When we'd finished I said, "Anything else?"

"No," said Morris. "Go'way."

The strange thing was that instead of feeling annoyed I couldn't help laugh, and he smiled at me.

Thankfully the rain had stopped by the time I turned into the alley with Gran's stuff. I'd have to go straight back out for our shopping after a cup of tea. My heart jumped when I saw Karuna coming out of Mr Banerjee's backyard. "Keep cool," I said to myself. I flicked back my wet hair, which was all over the place. "Hello," he said with a fab'lous smile.

I smiled and nodded – couldn't speak. *Good start,* I thought.

"I hope you've recovered after your nasty experience with your bike?"

"Oh, I'm OK," I managed to say.

"Popping in to see your grandmother?"

I nodded, stiff as a shop dummy. "Yes, she needs

help with the shopping an' such," I said, making out I was Saint Gemma of the Mawr. Cringe.

"Well, have a good day. Give my regards to Lilly."

There's posh, I thought. "Have a good day" and "give my regards". No one said things like that on the Mawr, least not if you're my age. "You too," I said. He walked away. "I like your playing ... your flute playing."

He turned. "Thank you. You and Lilly must say if it disturbs you."

"No. She likes it too." I was trying my best to be casual. "I've ... I've always wanted to play – the flute, I mean."

What a stinker of a lie that was.

He came back towards me. "Really? It's a beautiful instrument."

"Yes," I said, like I'd thought about it.

"I never get tired of playing. The sound reminds me of sunshine, and birds..."

I nodded. "Or a waterfall."

He smiled. "Yes." His eyes sparkled like jewels. "Does your school offer music lessons?"

"No," I said, without knowing for sure.

"Well, I'll see what I can do."

My mobile started ringing. "See you around," he said.

"Yes. Have a good day. Do give my regards to Mr Banerjee."

I watched him go with a stupid grin on my face, then answered the phone. "Yeah?"

"*That Gemma?*"

"Who's this?"

"*It's Kate... Got your number off your gran. Where are you?*"

"Alleyway behind the terrace."

"*Think I got your bike.*"

I burst into Gran's house. "Here's your shopping!"

She grinned at me. "Hope it's your bike, Gemma."

"Me too!"

I ran to the post office where Kate said she was. I could see her standing outside holding on to a bike. There was a man, looking well peeved, holding it too and Kate's mam, Kerry, stood beside them. I ran up, totally out of breath. It was my bike, all right. It wasn't just the scratches on the handlebars; I'd put a red mudguard on the back wheel that hadn't come with the bike when I bought it, so I was sure. When I explained that to the man, he said, "Well, anyone could come up and say that, couldn't they?"

"Where d'you buy it?" Kate asked him.

"A mate, all right?"

"Let's call the police," said Kerry. "See what they say."

"Wait a minute," the man said. "I paid money for this bike, legit."

"It was stolen," Kate said.

"I think the police should be informed," Kerry said calmly to the man.

He looked around nervously.

I took out the twenty pounds Mam had given me for the shopping. "You can have this," I said, desperate to have my bike back.

"No, Gemma. It was stolen," said Kate. "He's giving it back to you because it's yours." She looked at the bloke. "Aren't you?"

He pulled the twenty pounds from my hand. "Reward money." He let go of the bike and walked away.

"Hey!" Kate called after him.

"Doesn't matter," I said. "I got it back."

She looked at me – her eyes still angry.

I smiled at her. "That was brilliant, Kate. You're amazing."

"MAM!" I shouted. "Got my bike back!"

She came out of the kitchen. "Where was it?"

"Kate found it in town. Stopped a bloke on it.

Held him up and called me. Brilliant, she is."

"That's good."

"I gave the man the money, but it's all right..."

"You what?"

"I've got it, Mam. I got the twenty, but I gave it to him because, well, cheaper than buying a new bike, isn't it? I'll get the rest of the shopping now."

Mam went on at me as I went upstairs to get the money Gran had given me, but I was so happy I didn't care. I went straight back to the supermarket – didn't want to risk taking the bike. The sun came out like it was happy for me – corny I know, but I felt so good. I decided to ride up to the farm straight after and thank Kate properly.

Kate Thomas – cowgirl and bike-thief catcher of Wales.

Seventeen

I was free again. The sun was still out and the road was glinting wet, like silver. I was flying. I got to the top of the hill and lifted my arms. "YEEES!" I shouted as I gazed at the Bryn Mawr below. On the way down I screamed a happy scream as the wind battered me.

Kerry came out as I turned into the farmyard. "Hello, Gemma. Kate went off somewhere – didn't say where."

"Come to thank her, and you, for finding my bike."

"Lucky, wasn't it?" she said. "Kate just walked up to that man and said, 'This is my friend's bike.' Cool as a cucumber, she was."

I smiled – Kate calling me "friend".

"Come in for a cuppa," she said, "since you come all this way. Don't worry, no one'll steal your bike up here."

There was a lovely smell in the kitchen when I went in. I sat at the table as Kerry prepared the drink. "Hungry?"

"Yes, please, Mrs Thomas." My stomach agreed with a rumble.

"Oh, call me Kerry."

She came to the table with a plate of fruit cake. Stonking, it was – home-made. "Lovely," I said.

"You're a first, you know."

I stopped eating. "First what?"

"Never met one of Kate's friends before. I'm glad," she said. "She loves those cows, but she spends far too much time on her own. Sometimes I look at her and she seems grown up already."

She stared at me. I thought maybe she was amazed by the amount of cake I had in my mouth. "Does she talk to you?" she asked.

I nodded even though she didn't, not really.

"It's just that I know Kate doesn't want us to sell the cows, and I just wish she'd understand…"

I pushed more cake into my mouth so that I

wouldn't have to say anything.

"Those cows don't earn their keep," she said. "It's like Kate's got twelve pets. With the money we'd get we could pay off Mostyn – it'd give us a fresh start..."

It was like she was talking to herself rather than me. I glanced at the photograph of Kate's granddad. Kerry must have noticed.

"She loved her Gramps, and when he died she took it very badly, only natural. But two months later the foot-an'-mouth outbreak came along. Our cows didn't have the disease but the whole herd had to be culled as a precaution. Kate was devastated. She cried and cried. In the end we sent her off to stay with relatives while it all happened. When she came back she didn't speak for a month ... and I mean didn't speak at all."

She gazed out of the window. "Don't know why I'm telling you all this. I suppose it's because I've never met a friend of Kate's and she doesn't say a lot. She stormed out earlier – had a blazing row with her father."

She smiled at me. "D'you get on with your dad?"

There was no cake left, so I shrugged and took a gulp of tea to avoid answering.

"You were hungry."

I nodded, still a bit embarrassed. "D'you know a

place where there's a waterfall?" I said it before I'd thought it through.

"Sorry?"

"A waterfall and a big tree. The water pours down rocks and boulders..."

Which is what most waterfalls do, I thought. *Duh!*

"What's the name of the place?" Kerry asked.

"Don't know."

"Forestry Commission is probably your best bet, especially around here – lots of reservoirs and rivers and such."

I nodded. "Best get off."

"I'll tell Kate you dropped by. She'll be sorry she missed you."

As I started back down I wondered if Kate really would be sorry she missed me, or whether that was mam-talk. I passed by the field where the cows grazed and stopped by the gate. There they were, heads down chewing at the grass.

"Hello," I called. They ignored me. "Got my bike back, thanks to Kate." They went on chewing like they were on a time limit. I suppose they were – they're born, milked, killed and then eaten. I felt sorry for them.

It was lovely cycling back into the Mawr. I decided to go to Gran's and maybe offer to do something round the house. This time I'd lock my bike to the drainpipe, certain.

As I went through town I kept an eye open for Kate, but didn't see her. When I turned into the back alley there was a crowd all pressed round the doorway of Gran's backyard. I felt a rush of fear that something bad had happened.

"What's going on?" I asked as I pedalled up to them. There were even people looking over the neighbours' walls.

"Gran! Gran!"

"Lilly's fine, Gemma," said Polly, but she seemed worried so I wasn't convinced.

"Gran!" I shouted as I pushed through the crowd.

Then I saw a cow – a proper, real cow.

Eighteen

"It's Jane," Gran said to me. "Remember? Isn't she beautiful?"

I stared at the cow as Kate was filling a tin bath with fodder. There was a pile of hay on the ground. "What's it doing here?" I asked.

"Kate brought her down to see me."

"Oh, for the day, like?"

"No," said Gran. "Long as I like. Isn't that right?"

Kate shrugged her shoulders. "She'll probably be better cared for here than up there." She glanced up at the hills, as if the Thomas farm was round the corner. "If she's too much trouble I'll

take her back."

"It's bonkers!" said Roger.

"Don't you start!" said Gran. "It's my backyard. I'll do as I like."

"But what about the smell, the noise?" asked Roger.

"I have to put up with your smells and noises."

"What about food?" I asked.

Kate pointed at the tin bath. "That'll last a while. I can bring more if need be. Then there's grass, weeds, hay..."

"I'll go round and collect greenery for her," said Gran. "It'll keep me fit and I'll be doing this overgrown, shabby estate a favour."

"Oh Lilly, come on – a cow!" said Polly.

"How many cats have you got?"

"Only two. What are you saying, Lil? Two cats are as much bother as a great hulking cow?"

"No, I'm not saying that, course not, but this beauty will give me milk to drink, and I can make butter and cheese as well. All she wants is grass an' such. She'll earn her keep, not like cats who just want a feed and a snooze."

At this point Jane raised her tail and did a huge poo on to Gran's patio.

"Great," said Roger. "It's going to stink to high heaven round here!"

"I'll take it," said Mr Banerjee. "Manure for my roses. They'll grow well."

"There you are," said Gran. "Whenever Jane drops a load I'll let you know, Mr Banerjee. You can count on it."

"You won't have to tell him," said Roger. "He'll smell it!"

Everyone started chipping in about how stupid it was to have a cow in the backyard, and, to be honest, I had to agree.

"I don't care," said Gran, raising her hands in the air. "We've got plenty of real problems on the Bryn Mawr. You don't need me to tell you that. This cow, Jane, she won't be smashing your windows, or stealing, or shouting foul-mouthed abuse, or mugging you when you come back from the post office with your pension. No. She'll be good as gold, and give far more than she takes *and* she'll be company for me. So I ask you, give her a chance…"

Everyone went quiet.

Mr Banerjee joined his hands together. "She will bring us good luck."

"Thank you," said Gran, then the crowd parted and Morris walked up to Jane. I was surprised because he usually stays indoors.

"Lovely isn't she, Morris?" said Gran.

He stared at Jane. "I'll build her a shelter, if you want, Lilly," he said in a whisper.

"I think that's a cracking idea, Morris."

"Got a tarpaulin in the attic," he added. "Won't be fancy but it'll do the job."

Roger tutted. "A tarpaulin?"

"A simple shelter is all she needs, Roger," said Gran, "not the Great Wall of China. Thank you, Morris."

She turned to everyone. "Right. Show's over now. I want to settle Jane into her new home and milk her."

"Any milk left over, Lilly, I'll take it," Roger said.

"Oh, will you? Well, Morris'll be first as he's offered to put up the shelter. Now, if you don't mind…"

Gran started shooing them away as if they were pigeons.

I turned to Kate. "Went up the farm to see you, on my bike. Your mam said nothing about you taking a cow down to Gran."

She stared at me with her dad's scary eyes.

"That's because she doesn't know."

NINETEEN

"A cow!" Mam said, wide-eyed as she fried sausages. "This a joke?"

"It's true," said Darren. "Ryan told me – a dirty great cow in Gran's yard. Can we go see it?"

"Whose big idea was this then?"

"The Cowgirl, Mam. The nutter I told you about," said Darren.

"Kate brought her down to her, temporary like."

"Oh, I promise you that it's temporary. I want that cow gone yesterday."

I didn't like the way Mam was treating Gran like she did me. "Mam, it's her choice."

"Choice? I'll go round tomorrow and talk sense into her," she said as she shook her head. The sausages were spitting, just like she was spitting mad. "Maybe she had a funny turn when Ruby died – I mean, a whole cow. Costs money, you know, keeping a cow."

"Yeah," I said. "Grass is so pricey these days."

"Don't be sarky, Gemma. This is your doing."

"Me? I didn't know till today."

"You got your gran the invite to the farm, though, didn't you?"

"No Mam, Kate did."

"Well, Kate can take her cow back."

She came to the table and plonked a couple of sausages dripping in oil on each of our plates. I pictured Jane with her big, staring eyes.

"I'll just have beans, Mam," I said.

"Don't start, Gemma. I'm not in the mood."

"Honest now, Mam, I don't want them."

"Why not?"

It was bad timing, but right at that moment I realised.

"I want to be vegetarian from now on."

TWENTY

Sunday morning Gran didn't answer the door.

"Maybe she's round the back with Jane," I said to Mam.

"Who's Jane?"

"The cow," I said.

Mam clucked her tongue. "I can't be bothered going round," she said. "Go and open up for me."

I started walking and Darren followed.

"Got your bike back then?" he said with a smirk.

"Yeah. Got a cut of the money, did you?"

"No!"

We turned into the alley and I could see people at

Gran's back door again. "That'll never do the job," Roger was saying, looking up at Morris leaning out of Gran's upstairs window. He was tying the corner of a blue tarpaulin to a hook on the wall.

"Where's Gran?" I asked.

"Indoors, making cheese," said Roger.

"Massive!" said Darren, staring at Jane. "A proper, massive cow."

"Be careful you don't annoy her or she'll turn on you," Roger said. "Dangerous, cows are. Killed people, they have."

"No, they haven't," said Darren.

Right on cue, Jane turned and eyeballed him. He backed away and I couldn't help smiling.

"What are you scared of, Darren?" I said. "It's a cow not a crocodile."

It was out before I realised it's what Kate had first said to me. Then I heard Gran's doorbell. "Oh! Forgot about Mam!"

I went into the back of the house, and there was Gran stirring something in a huge bowl. "Gran, Mam's at the door!"

"Oh, Gemma, I haven't stopped," she said. "What with the milking, making cheese here, then clearing out the yard..."

"Well, take it easy, Gran," I said.

"Why should I? I haven't enjoyed myself this much since the war. Oh, by the by, Mr Banerjee's grandson dropped that off for you." She nodded towards the sideboard, and I noticed a black case.

"What is it?"

"A flute. Said you'd always fancied learning to play. News to me."

I opened the case and saw a lovely silver flute in two sections.

"Takes lots of practice, Gemma," said Gran. "He said he'd give you a lesson sometime."

I felt all warm hearing that; then I heard Mam knocking loudly.

"Oh, let her in for goodness' sake," said Gran. "That door won't take much more."

"Gran, don't tell Mam about the flute," I said.

"Right you are," she replied as she stirred the cheese. I loved the way Gran didn't question some things. I went through and opened the front door.

"Where you been?" Mam said as she entered.

"Sorry, Mam, got distracted."

On the pavement was a man, woman and two children. "This where the cow is?" he asked.

"Yes," I said, but I wondered if they were inspectors or something.

"Do you think we could show the kids? Bit of a

novelty, like."

"I'll ask," I said.

Gran was still stirring the cheese as I came back. "People at the door, Gran, asking if they can see Jane."

"Course they can. Bring 'em through."

Mam came in from the yard. "Of all the stupid things I've seen in my life, Mam. Come on now, a great, lumping cow in your backyard. I mean, what for?"

"Milk, butter, cheese and company," said Gran.

"Company? Talking cow, is it?"

"No. And don't call her 'lumping' – sensitive, she is. Anyway," she muttered, "pot calling the kettle black."

I went to the front door and invited the family in. I took them through the kitchen where Mam was still having a go at Gran.

"It's a liability, Mam!"

"How?"

"How? It's a cow, that's how!"

"Ooh, that rhymes," Gran said to herself with a chuckle, then she noticed the family. "Oh, hello. Come to see Jane, have you?"

"If it's no trouble," he said. "I'm John and this is my wife, Mary, and the kids; we're the Llewellyns from over the Common."

"No trouble at all, love. She's out back. Follow me." Gran led them out.

"We're thinking of getting some chickens," he said as he passed us. "Bit of sustainable living."

"She's letting strangers through the house," Mam said to me, just as thumping footsteps came down the stairs and Morris walked by on his way out.

"What was he doing upstairs?" Mam asked.

"Fixing up a shelter for Jane."

I've never seen Mam look so surprised. "She's got a cow in the backyard, she's making cheese in a bucket, and a nutter roaming around upstairs. She's lost her ruddy marbles!"

Mam went to the back door. I stood beside her and we watched as Gran showed Jane to the visiting family. Morris and Roger were still arguing as they fixed the tarpaulin to the back wall and Mr Banerjee was shovelling cow dung into a bucket.

"Any going spare?" Mr Llewellyn asked him.

"Yes, certainly," he replied.

"Hello, Mr Banerjee," I said.

He smiled at me. "Hello, Gemma."

He had a nice, kind smile, and I wondered why I'd ever avoided him.

Darren came running in from the back alley. "This

do, Gran?"

He was holding a load of grass and weeds.

"That'll do lovely, Darren."

"Can I feed her?"

"Aye, she likes fresh grass and such."

I watched my annoying, creeping, sly little brother start feeding grass to Jane, like he was a country boy. I was amazed. I looked at Mam, but she was still staring open-mouthed at Mr Banerjee shovelling cow poo. Darren was grinning as Jane chewed away at the grass he'd brought her. "There's loads out back, Gran," he said. "I'll get some more."

"Good boy, Darren! Good boy!"

"I don't believe it," said Mam. I was about to say "nor do I" when I noticed the shrub I helped Gran plant over Ruby and realised she hadn't mentioned that dog for ages. Now she had a backyard full of people, and she was busy and happy.

"Due for a milking, aren't you, girl?" Gran said to Jane. "Gemma. D'you fancy milking her?" she asked. "You seen me do it."

I surprised myself when I said, "Go on then."

Twenty One

The teats were warm. Gran taught me to pinch the top of the teat with my thumb and squeeze with my fingers. I got the hang of it eventually. Jane turned her head and gave me a look, as if she was saying, "Not bad, now just get on with it." It was awesome to see milk squirt out, and it wasn't long before the bucket was almost full. Then Ryan and Jamie walked in, bold as brass.

"Who said you could waltz in here?" said Roger, as he was fixing the tarpaulin with Morris.

"Come to see the cow, 'aven't we?" said Ryan.

"Right, well, there she is. Now hop it!"

"You can stay if you behave," said Gran.

"Massive, innit?" said Jamie.

"Watch it! She's milking," said Darren. "Dangerous, she is now. Trample you to death if you're not careful."

"Crap," said Ryan, as he stepped back.

"What's that coming out?" asked Jamie, pointing at the bucket.

"Milk, of course!" Gran said. "Have your cornflakes dry, do you?"

Roger laughed, and so did Mr Banerjee.

"Where d'you think it came from then?"

Jamie and Ryan stared at the milk squirting into the bucket like they'd just been told they'd eaten chips made with maggots.

"It's heated up," Gran explained. "Otherwise it could make you ill. It has to be pasteurised, like in the supermarket."

Jamie covered his mouth and ran out into the alley.

Loads of people were popping round to gawp at Jane in the backyard. I thought it was funny, because, let's face it, if you want to see a cow you can go out into the country – there's loads of them – but put one in a backyard on the Bryn Mawr and it was like a celebrity had turned up.

Mam paced the kitchen as Gran stirred the milk in a

huge pot she had on the cooker.

"I'm worried, Mam, I got to say."

"I can tell," said Gran. "Is it Robbie?"

Robbie's my dad.

"No, Mam, it's not Rob. It's you!"

"Me?" Gran winked at me.

"Yes, Mam. I mean, I know you must be sad losing Ruby an' all, but a cow?"

"That cow has nothing to do with Ruby. Kate asked me if I fancied looking after her for a while and I jumped at the chance."

"And did this Kate give you money to look after her?"

Gran stopped stirring the milk. "Now, listen here," she said. "What I do in this house is my business, right? That cow's not cost me a penny so far…"

Darren came in with his hands full of grass. "Gran! This all right? Got it from Morris's garden, said we were doing him a favour." Jamie and Ryan were behind him.

"Spoil her, you will," Gran said with a grin. "Go on, be gentle."

I went to the back door – I just didn't trust them, but there they were, the three of them, feeding the cow what they'd pulled up from Morris's backyard.

"Don't go on, love," said Gran to Mam when I

came back. "I'm having fun. And if you're worried about the money I let you have each week, don't. I'll still help you out."

This was news to me. I had no idea Gran was subbing her.

"It's not that," Mam said. "I'm just worried about the strain it'll put on you."

"You just concentrate on you and I'll look after me, right?"

"But how long are you going to keep it?"

Gran took a tin out of a cupboard. She pulled out the tea bags, and then from the bottom a couple of twenty-pound notes. "I'll keep *her* as long as Kate lets me," she said as she handed Mam some money. "And by the way." She glanced at me. "Your daughter's been a marvellous help. A star, she is."

I blushed.

Twenty Two

When I turned into the farmyard the sun was going down so I knew I'd have to head back pretty soon, but I wanted to see Kate and tell her all that was going on. I could see a light on in the milking shed, and, sure enough, there she was, splashing the floor with water and brushing it away.

"Hi," I shouted.

She frowned as she came up to me, looking over my shoulder like she was checking who was around. "Everything all right?"

"Everything's great. The neighbours have got into Jane too, even my brother, Darren. Gran's got them

all running round for her."

Kate went back to washing down.

"I milked her!" I said. "With my hands, I milked Jane."

She nodded and I think I saw a little smile. A car came into the farmyard and her head snapped up. It was her dad.

He came straight across to the shed, and gave me a nod.

"Everything all right?" he asked Kate.

"Why shouldn't it be?"

"Talking to Don Mostyn just now..." he said.

Kate stopped sweeping.

"He wants to come and look over the cows. I told him they're in good shape and gave the credit to you."

I shouldn't have been there by rights but it was like my shoes were cemented to the ground.

"Be a new start, Kate. There'll be enough money left over to buy a shredder, so I can do some proper tree surgery and garden clearance. I'm going to set up a workshop in here, and then—"

"Can I keep one of the cows?" Kate asked, stopping him dead in his tracks.

"What? What for?"

She was gripping the sweeping brush so tight her fingers were white. "I wanna keep one."

"What's the point?"

"I want a cow."

She said it like she was asking for new clothes or a mobile. Her dad glanced at me. "We need all the money we can get."

"I'll buy one off you. You can take it out of my pocket money – pay you back a little at a time."

"Kate, don't try me."

"A cow loan."

"That's enough!"

"That's right. You've had enough and given up."

"No. You're just blind to what's happening in the real world of farming. You're great with those cows, a natural. But you're thirteen – you know nothing about milk quotas, or wholesale prices, inspection costs, vaccination costs. You just see this farm like … like you're looking at a picture book – Jack and Jill go to the farm. You'd have us prancing around pretending to be a farm, because that's what we're doing, just pretending!" He turned and walked out.

Kate went up to the door, staring after him as if I wasn't there. She looked like she hated him. "He still hasn't spotted one's missing."

She let the brush fall to the floor and left. I watched her disappear into the darkness. I was going to be late back, but she was in far worse trouble.

❀❀❀

Mam was watching the TV when I got in. I'd phoned as I left the farm – said I had a puncture, just as an excuse. She was still angry by the time I got home.

"Sorry, Mam," I said.

"I don't want be on the front of the *Echo*, Gemma – *Mother lets thirteen-year-old daughter stay out all night.*"

"Had to stop every five minutes to pump up my tyre."

"New inner tube," said Darren.

"There's your dinner," said Mam, with a wave at the table.

There was a pork chop, potatoes and veg. I didn't react. I was too hungry. I ate the potatoes and veg in a couple of mouthfuls. Mam was watching the TV, but I could sense her looking at me now and again.

"Gran said cows have got four stomachs," said Darren. "Four!"

Mam grunted.

"Jane ate tons and tons of grass."

"It's a cow, Darren," Mam said. "It's not Jane, it's a cow."

"People call their pets names, Mam, don't they?"

"It's not a pet, though, is it? It's a cow, for God's sake! What you two don't get is that it's difficult enough for me to make ends meet without my eighty-year-old mam looking after a cow!"

"She's got loads of help," said Darren. "Me and Jamie are helping too."

"If you want to help you could tidy your room, do your own washing and get dinner underway, yeah? Charity begins at home. Ever heard of that?"

"No. What's it mean?"

I couldn't help smile.

"It's not funny, Gemma!"

"Mam, it's not forever," I said. "She's happy being so busy, and she was so sad when Ruby died."

"I never would have thought I'd say it but I wish that dog was still alive."

"I don't," said Darren and me at the same time.

"You two been sponsored to disagree with me or something? And are you going to eat that pork chop?" she asked me.

"No, Mam. I'm veggie now. It'll save you money, won't it? Whatever vegetables you cook I'll eat."

Mam shook her head.

"Hey!" said Darren. "We can tell Dad about Jane tomorrow!"

It was a bank holiday and I'd forgotten about visiting Dad.

"I'm sure he'll be fascinated," said Mam. She

sighed. "I don't know, a useless bloke in prison and a mam with a cow in her backyard – 'appy days."

Later, when I was in my room, I tried the flute for the first time. But all I could get out of it was a stupid hooting noise.

"*Gemma!*" Mam shouted. "*What the hell's that noise?*"

"Nothing!" I yelled back.

I looked at the lovely silver tube and said to myself, "It's just a flute I'll never be able to play."

Twenty Three

We sat facing Dad at a table among the other prisoners with visitors. I never felt comfortable being there. All the prisoners met their visitors in the same room. I hated that – sometimes you'd see people crying or having an argument, and it was tense all the time.

Dad was looking fit and well, though his hair was in a ponytail which was well embarrassing.

"Should see her," said Darren. "Massive, she is."

"What's this?" Dad asked.

"What he says – a cow at my mam's."

"Joke, is it?"

"No."

"Looking well, Claire," he said to Mam.

"Well, it's all the sun I'm getting, and restaurant food."

Mam's sark bounced off him. "In the gym all the time now," he said, "and I'm up to a hundred press-ups."

It irritated me that he didn't ask about the cow – it's not like you hear someone's got a cow in their backyard every day.

"She makes cheese and butter too," said Darren.

"Who does?"

"Gran, with the milk from Jane."

"Who's Jane?"

"The cow," I said. "All the neighbours are helping out, even Morris."

Dad nodded, but I could tell he wasn't interested. "Hundred sit-ups too – rock hard, my stomach," he said as he slapped his belly. "You'll be well impressed, Claire. New man for you when I'm out."

"Can't wait. What's his bank balance like?"

"Course I need loads of protein. So when I'm out I'll be eating this cow."

He laughed, but me and Darren didn't.

"Your daughter's a veggie now," said Mam.

"What? Won't last long."

"I am, Dad. Don't want to eat animals any more."

I felt proud, like I was announcing it to everyone.

"You will if you're hungry enough."

"No, I won't."

He was beginning to annoy me.

"I'll bet you a tenner you'll eat a burger by the time I get out."

"Robbie," said Mam. "Betting got you into enough trouble without you betting with your own daughter."

"I'm only saying, love. I'm on your side."

"There's no sides, Rob. When you get out you'll be back in the real world, and you'll have to earn your keep – a bit like Jane."

"Who's Jane?"

"The COW!"

TWENTY FOUR

"On your own, Cowgirl number two?" said Sian as she got on the bus. "I heard about your gran taking on a cow – runs in the family then."

It was odd but I didn't feel at all bothered by her. I suppose there were more important things to worry about. I imagined Jane stood in the yard, steam coming from her nostrils and Gran hunched over as she milked her, and I wondered if Kate's dad knew one of the cows was missing yet.

The bus arrived at school, and as everyone started getting off I remembered what Kate had told me once about cows behaving funny when they're taken to slaughter, like they know something's up. Kate told me horses get put out to pasture, which is like retirement – eating, sleeping and galloping around; but not cows – they're killed and sliced up for burgers or dog food.

"Ignoring me?" Sian said, her face shoved into mine. "Cowgirl's learning you fast, isn't she?"

"Cows get a rotten life, you know," I said. She looked puzzled. "Well, I mean, all they do is eat grass, and when they have a calf it's taken away as soon as it's born, so the cow still gives out milk, see, which we take for ourselves."

"So?"

"That's a rotten life, don't you reckon?"

"Not bothered."

"No. Suppose you're not. Not many are."

"You trying to be funny?"

"No. Are you?"

I wanted to go, and as I stepped forward she backed off, which I thought was funny. I laughed, and then she grabbed me.

Right in the middle of all the shouting and screaming I realised how stupid fighting was. She was clawing and hitting me, I was doing the same back, and to be honest it didn't hurt. It was just … well, as I said, stupid. Sian was no stronger than me.

She was vicious and angry. I was angry too, but I had reason, and right at that moment I took everything out on her. By the time a teacher turned up it was me on top of Sian, hitting and clawing. When he pulled me off I could feel my eye swelling.

I stared at Sian and saw nothing but a nasty bully, and I knew I wasn't scared of her any more.

"It's a misunderstanding, sir," I said to the teacher. "I was just telling Sian what a rotten life cows have, what with being killed so young just for burgers and such. She thought I was talking about her, but I wasn't. I was talking about cows and how brilliant they are." The kids around us started giggling. "They give us their milk and all the thanks they get is being slaughtered before they even get into Year One!"

I think they thought I'd lost it, but I was in control and Sian knew it.

Kate was a no-show that morning and I was itching to know what was happening, so at lunchtime I ran out of school and across the Common to Gran's. Her back door was shut. I went round and knocked on the front door, but there was no answer. The curtain moved aside and Roger looked out at me. Then the door opened and Kate was standing there. "D'you get my text?"

"No."

"What happened to your eye?"

"Doesn't matter. What's going on?"

Kate glanced into the street. "Come in."

When I went into the lounge there was Mr Banerjee, Morris, Roger, Polly, Mr Llewellyn and loads of people I didn't know. They all had cups of tea and were gathered around Gran in her armchair, like she was the queen. She asked about my eye, so I told her about the fight.

"Good for you," she said, which made me smile. "We been waiting for you, Gemma. Fancy some cheese, courtesy of Jane?" Whatever was going on it had nothing to do with cheese tasting.

"We been talking," said Gran. "Kate's dad knows a cow is missing now."

"I told him," said Kate. "He blew his top. Got straight on the phone to Don Mostyn and cut a deal. He'll be coming to collect 'em any day."

I had a brainwave. "Gran. Why don't you buy Jane?"

"Thought of that, love," she replied. "Well over a grand, a good cow like Jane is worth. I haven't got that kind of money. Wish I had."

"What'll Mostyn do with them?" I asked.

"He'll take 'em into his herd, calf them once or

twice maybe, and then straight to slaughter. He just wants his field back and the money he's owed."

"The miser," said Roger.

"I love having that cow here," said Gran, "and so do the neighbours." She nodded to the others, who all started talking.

"Lovely cheese she makes," said Roger with his mouth full.

"She brings us peace," said Mr Banerjee.

"Aye," agreed Morris.

"The cream I made from that milk was like nothing I've ever tasted," said Polly.

It went quiet and I couldn't bear it. "So? What's happ'ning?"

"Well," said Gran, "they don't know where Jane is as yet, so we decided, or Kate has suggested, that we take the rest."

"How d'you mean, the rest?"

"We want the whole dozen down here, on the estate. It's all hush-hush though."

I stood there gobsmacked. "You want to bring eleven cows down here," I asked. "On to the Bryn Mawr?"

"That's right. We've got takers for every single one," said Gran. "We didn't say anything before, as we wanted to be absolutely sure. So we put the word out, and this morning Kate and I interviewed all those interested to make sure they were serious and had enough room in their back gardens or yards. In the end, we had so many takers we had to draw lots. We've got a good home for every cow. We're going to hide them, Gemma. Hide them until we can find a long-term solution to help Mr Thomas. We want those cows to live longer and happier – a lot longer than Mostyn will keep 'em alive."

I couldn't believe they were serious.

"You can't hide twelve cows on the Bryn Mawr estate!"

"Why not?" said Roger.

"But how you going to get 'em down?"

"Same way that I got Jane here," said Kate. "I know a route that'll take us all the way to the bridge over the motorway. There's a field just past that, then we'll take 'em to their new homes a few at a time."

"But they'll be spotted. Someone might tell."

"Tell what?" said Gran. "I saw a cow in town? Unless one of them goes into a shop for a pint of milk no one'll care."

"When are you thinking of doing it?"

"Tomorrow."

"Tomorrow?"

"Yeah, and I'll need your help, Gemma," said Kate.

"It'll be safer and quieter on a school day. Will you do it?"

They all stared at me. "I think you're all bonkers," I said. "Mad, you are…"

I thought of my fight with Sian and the anger everywhere. I realised I'd prefer to be bonkers than angry.

"Yeah, let's do it!"

That night I was trying out the flute, and for the first time I managed to get a decent sound out of it. Then Darren came in. "Get out!"

"I wanna go," he said.

I held the flute at arm's length. "No."

"Not on that. I want to go with you and help with the cows tomorrow."

"What you on about?" I said, pretending I didn't know what he meant.

"Don't mess, Gem. I heard Roger talking. All the cows are coming down on to the Mawr."

"Darren. You got to be in school."

"But you won't be, why can't I?"

"Because if I don't show we'll get away with it, but not both of us."

"I'll tell Mam."

I sat up. "Look you, if you mess up this mission…"

I couldn't believe I called it a mission. "If you mess this up, Gran will lose Jane."

"I won't … I won't…"

"Then stay out of it."

"No. I wanna help."

"Why?"

I can't remember the last time I saw my brother looking bashful, but there he was, stood at the end of my bed with his eyes on the floor. "John Wayne," he said.

"Who?"

"I was watching a film about these boys on horses moving cattle. John Wayne was teaching 'em."

"We haven't got horses."

"We got bikes. Go on, Gem. I'll be a help, I will. Go on!"

"Darren, if Mam finds out…"

"She won't. Thanks, Gem."

"Darren!"

He was gone.

TWENTY FIVE

I didn't sleep a wink, and during breakfast Mam wanted to know why we were so quiet.

"Tired," Darren and me said. She stared at us, which made me think she'd sussed something was up.

When we got our bikes outside I saw Jamie at the end of our road. "Darren, tell him we got to pick up something for Mam. Get rid of him."

"He's coming with us."

"What? You told him?"

"He'll help, Gemma."

"All right," I said. "You can both help."

"Lush!"

"If you can keep up."

I started in low gear for acceleration, and ten seconds later they were specks in the distance behind me. If Darren was going to open his big mouth he got what he deserved.

I pushed up Craig-y-Nos hill like I'd never done before. I didn't want to let Kate down. I'd arranged to meet her at the gate at the far end of the field, where the cows grazed.

I was early. I stood there on my own, the breath coming out my mouth like a steam train. It was quiet; that sort of quiet you don't often get, like the time I lay in the middle of the road. No cars, nothing; just a bird singing as if it was in a competition. Lovely, it was. Then I thought about Dad in his cell. "Stupid," I said out loud.

I heard a moo.

"C'mon," I heard Kate call out. "Get along!"

The cows came into sight and there was Kate, riding on the back of one of them like a real cowgirl. I laughed. She saw me and smiled, but I could tell she was nervous too. She got off the cow, opened the gate and stepped into the lane.

"Quiet, isn't it?" I said.

Kate gazed around. "They been milked and fed.

I'll lead them, you follow at the back."

"What do I have to do?"

"Nothing. Just keep them from stopping."

"What if they turn around?"

"They won't. They might get distracted by grass at the side of the lane but they'll follow the others. When I hold them up at the front they'll all stop. When you see us moving off just clap your hands and shout 'Get along' and they'll move."

I wanted to ask, "What if they don't?" But I knew it wouldn't help.

Kate glanced up and down the lane. "OK. Let's go."

She went back into the field and my heart started thumping.

"Go on!" she shouted. "GO ON!"

"What? Go where?"

"NOT YOU!" she yelled. "The cows! You just stay there!"

They started coming out into the lane, giving me the scary eye. They all followed each other, except one that turned towards me. "Go on!" I said in a thin voice. "Get along!" I clapped. Nothing. The cow glared at me, then mooed. Petrified, I was.

"Get along!"

She mooed again, like she was saying, "Who are

you to tell me where to go?"

The last cow came out and Kate closed the gate. "That's Rachel. Stubborn, she is. Shout at her like you shout at your brother."

"Rachel," I said. "Get along!"

"That's not how you talk to your brother."

The cow stared at me and I got annoyed. "GET ALONG! GET!"

She turned and joined the others.

"That's the way," said Kate.

She made her way through them. "Come on, girls!" she shouted, and they all started to move off down the lane. I followed, looking at the bums of the last three cows. Now and again I'd shout, "Get!" or "Go on!" just because it made me feel like I was a proper cowgirl too.

It wasn't long before Kate called out, "Coming up to a crossroads. Keep 'em moving!"

We got through OK and on we went, but at the next crossroads a car pulled up. The driver wound down the window. "Where you off with them, Kate?"

Kate stayed back as the cows carried on. "Bit of exercise, Mr Jarvis."

"Shouldn't you be at school?"

"Yeah, taking these down for 'Bring an' tell'."

Kate walked on. As I passed, the driver said, "Is she

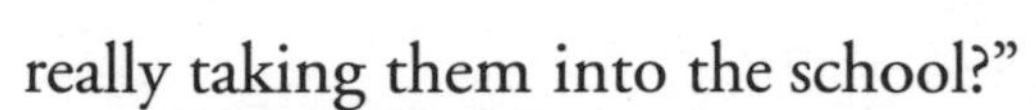

really taking them into the school?"

"That's right. Not into the classroom though. That would be ridic'lous, wouldn't it?"

We stopped for a break and the cows started chewing at the grass verges. Kate came through them. "All right?"

"Yeah," I said. "Going OK, isn't it?"

She nodded. I pulled out a chocolate bar I'd stashed. I broke it in two and handed half to Kate. "Chocolate always tastes better when you've saved it up," I said.

Kate bit into it. "They're enjoying it," she said, as she stroked the nearest cow.

"Which one's that?"

"Donna. Bit slow is Donna – she's easily scared. I'm putting her with Morris."

That's nice, I thought.

Just then there was a car horn. Kate looked at me. "If that's Dad, it's over." She went forward and I followed, even though I had to push through the cows.

"Kate. What's going on here?" the driver said.

"They got out, Mr Conway. Boys from the Mawr, we reckon. If you back up I'll get 'em past you."

"But you need to go that way, don't you?" He

pointed the way we'd come.

"There's no passing bay," said Kate. "You back up and we'll get 'em past you."

"There's kind of you, girl."

He reversed his car.

"Close one," she said to me. "Get 'em moving."

Once we were past the driver, he waved at us and drove on.

Not long after that we were at the motorway bridge, and there was Darren and Jamie waiting for us.

Twenty Six

"What you doing here?"

"Waiting for you!"

"You should be in school."

"So should you," said Darren. "You left us."

"Should've kept up."

We started arguing.

"Quiet!" said Kate. "We got eleven cows to take into the Bryn Mawr. There's a field just over this bridge. They can graze there and then we'll take a few at a time on to the Mawr. You either help or push off."

Darren and Jamie nodded their heads.

"Right. Let's go."

"Wagons roll!" shouted Darren as we started over the bridge.

I took up the rear, Darren and Jamie either side and Kate at the front.

It was funny, seeing all those cars zooming towards Swansea, or the other way to London, and eleven cows plodding across the motorway high above them as if they were saying, "What's your rush?"

It was a relief getting them into the field. It was overgrown and had an abandoned, burned-out car in the middle, but the cows were hungry and they started tucking into the grass straight away. We watched them for a while.

"Wish I was on a horse," said Darren.

Kate checked her watch. "Right, we'll tether them and take them down in two trips. One of you needs to stay here – I don't want them injuring themselves on any sharp objects. Darren, you stay. You get to watch over six cows. Reckon you can do it?" He nodded. "Right. We'll take Rachel, Connie, Megan, Suzie and Bess first."

All five were tethered. Jamie was given Megan. I was given Connie and Bess. They chewed grass, and now and again they'd lift their huge heads and glare at me. I talked to them to cover my nerves.

"We'll be off soon – off to your new homes."

"Be firm with them," Kate said. "Darren, just make sure the others don't go near that car and check the ground for metal and stuff they might hurt themselves on."

"Right," he said as he started looking around. Keen, he was. I realised that this was the first thing we were doing together without being forced. I remembered the time at the waterfall. He glanced at me, like he heard my thoughts. "Watch my bike, Darren," I said.

"OK."

I gave him a nod.

"Let's go," said Kate. "Keep encouraging them and they'll follow."

We were off. Once we'd got on to the road I could see the back end of the High Street up ahead, and people. I was nervous but Kate just marched along.

Cars had to wait to pull out and get around us, but no one seemed bothered. I thought of Mam at work and what would happen if we turned a corner and there she was. I imagined her face screwed up in anger.

"Keep 'em tight to the side," said Kate.

I snapped out of my thoughts. My heart was going like a machine gun. Somehow I expected police cars screeching to a stop in front of us. "You're under arrest for taking cows into town."

Kate was so cool. When we started passing people she'd just nod at them. I glanced at Connie and Bess, their heads bobbing up and down with the effort of walking. They weren't scary. It was silly to have ever thought that. I felt excited for them, escaping the slaughterhouse and going to new homes.

We came to a crossing with traffic lights. Kate pressed the button and we waited. A couple of elderly ladies stood with us – us and five cows. One of them turned to Kate and said, "These the girls for the Bryn Mawr?"

"Yeah," said Kate.

They already knew. Word had got around – no surprise. The lady smiled. "My neighbour, Mrs Evans, she's getting one. She'll look after it well. Said she'd let me have some of the milk now and again."

"Nothing like fresh cow's milk," said the other lady.

The crossing beeps started. "Come on, girls," I said, and we crossed. I gave one of the waiting drivers a nod, like it was every day I crossed the High Street with five cows.

"Where you off with them then?" a man asked, crossing from the other side.

"The cows are coming home," Kate replied.

It was great. I loved it.

We'd got past the busiest part of the route, and now we were on the Mawr estate.

The first drop-off was Megan to Mr Llewellyn.

"Welcome, Megan," he said when we arrived. "I've built a pen for her – a cow sty, I suppose you could say." He laughed.

"Plenty of hay. That's good," Kate said. "She won't need milking again until this evening. Any problems, call Lilly and she'll get hold of me."

"Right you are."

Kate suddenly seemed unsure. "Well ... we need to deliver the rest."

We moved off and Mr Llewellyn waved goodbye. "He'd better look after her," I said, which is what I reckon Kate was thinking.

Soon we arrived at Mr and Mrs Evans's. "See you, Bess," I said, as I handed her over.

"Hello, Bess love," said Mrs Evans cheerily, but Mr Evans looked moody.

"This is madness," he said.

"Pay no heed," she said to us.

"But it's not legal, is it?" he asked.

"They're my cows," said Kate. "I'm giving them to you, temporary like. If there's a problem..."

"Oh no, there's no problem, love," said Mrs Evans. She glared at her husband. "You agreed, Ron. I want this cow and she's staying. I put up with your smoking, your beer and your betting. You're going to accept this cow or you can cook and clean for yourself. Understood?"

"Yes, dear," he mumbled. Well told off, he was.

We went on to take Connie to Maria Bracchi. She used to own a café on the High Street. Italian, she is.

"Oh, *che bella,*" she said.

"Her name's Connie," I said.

"No love, '*bella*' means pretty in Italian. She need milking yet?"

"Not till this afters," said Kate. "I'll be back later and show you how."

"Oh, I'll manage. I worked on a farm in Italy when I was your age, and besides, I had a little practice on Lilly's cow."

We dropped Rachel off with Mrs Oleski. She was Polish, had a couple of kids, and baked her own bread, according to Kate.

Lastly we dropped Suzie off with Mr and Mrs Choudary. He was an accountant, and she was a dressmaker. Their son and daughter were in our school.

"We work from home, so she'll always have company."

They seemed nice. Then we were stood in the

street, empty-handed.

"That's it," said Kate. "The rest are for the terrace." She checked her watch. "And we're still on schedule, but school will be out for lunch in half an hour so we'll wait until they go back."

Kate phoned Gran to tell her as we made our way back to the field. Part of me expected the rest of the cows to be gone when we got there, but Darren was watching over them like a shepherd.

Kate turned to Jamie. "Right, listen you. Thanks for your help but I want you to go back to school."

"What?"

"Too many of us out. Go back. We can manage these six, the three of us."

"Aww!"

"Go!" she said. Jamie picked up his bike and went without a word. Kate seemed to have power over people.

She sat down on the grass and leaned against a tree. She sighed. Something was wrong.

Twenty Seven

I sat down beside Kate, even though the grass was wet. "It's going well," I said.

" 'Cept it's hardly a secret! Those ladies at the crossing knew all about it."

"Yeah," I said. "Word gets around."

Kate stroked the head of one of the cows near to her as it chewed grass. "That Mr Evans was right," she said. "It *is* a mad idea."

I glanced at Darren, who was with one of the cows on the other side of the field. We didn't argue so much now, and he was helping out. I felt different too, and I knew it was mainly because of Kate and

the cows, but now it seemed she was regretting the whole thing.

"But we'll be saving them from slaughter. You said yourself that they've got years of life left in them. And if it wasn't for Mostyn..."

She pulled at the grass and didn't reply.

"Which one's this?" I asked, pointing at the cow in front of us.

"Rhiannon."

"Who's she going to?"

"Roger."

Rhiannon lifted her huge head and had a sniff of me. "Bad luck, Rhiannon." Her nose was all wet, and her warm breath came out like she was sighing and agreeing with me. I pulled a wad of grass and offered it. Her big, slimy tongue caught my hand as she took it.

"Dad's going to be fuming," Kate muttered.

"But he says the cows don't earn you any money."

"Doesn't mean to say he won't be fuming when he finds out they're all gone. And it's not going to take long for him to hear where they are."

"We can keep a secret on the Mawr if we need to."

Kate's second thoughts made me feel edgy. "What about your granddad? What d'you think he would've done?"

She shrugged. "Maybe he would have carried on and it would have been all right. Maybe he would have made it worse. He couldn't have stopped the foot-an'-mouth outbreak. I remember Granddad talking about it. I was a baby then. Farmers didn't just lose the cows, they lost all the milk those cows would have given if they'd lived – thousands of litres. So when the second outbreak came, after he died, I knew what it would mean for us. It wasn't Dad's fault, but I was angry because I thought he didn't care."

"Didn't care about the cows being killed, you mean?"

She nodded. "They sent me away, while it was sorted. I lost it big time..."

She was staring straight ahead like she was seeing it all happen again.

"I didn't want to go to my aunt in Monmouth. It felt like I was leaving the cows when they needed me. I remember Dad had to hold me while he tried to open the truck. You can still see the dent now where I kicked the door..."

Rhiannon stopped chewing, as if she was listening.

"When they brought me back to the farm the cows were gone. There was a massive circle of black on the ground where they'd been burned. I could smell

it in the air. Dad said it was my imagination, but it wasn't. It was there, a horrible stink that didn't go away. There's times I can still smell it."

We sat in silence. I didn't know what to say. It was like I was getting bigger and more confident and Kate was shrinking. "He tries hard, my dad," she said.

"My dad's in prison," I blurted out.

She nodded, like it was every day she heard people say that.

I pictured the waterfall and Dad showing us how to do a handstand. I saw his grin, full of mischief. "He used to take us out on trips." I made it sound like we went every weekend, but I guess I wanted to sound like a normal family. "He took us to that waterfall," I said. "D'you know it?"

I looked at her, hoping she would.

"Waterfall?"

"Yeah. It's around here someplace, and there's a field with a big tree."

She wasn't taking the bait.

"How can I find it?"

She shrugged. "Ordnance Survey?"

"What's that?"

"It's a map."

"But I don't know where the place is."

"You said there was a stream and a waterfall, not

far from here."

"Yeah."

"Well, everything like hills and streams will all be marked on the Ordnance Survey maps – process of elimination."

"But where can I get them?"

"We got some."

"Will you..." I so didn't want her to say no. "Will you help me?"

"OK."

I couldn't look at her, as I could feel tears well up in my eyes. "Thanks."

"Is your dad in prison for long?"

"He'll be out next month."

I remembered him with his ponytail sitting opposite us. "Stupid," I muttered. "My brother thinks he's great. Hero in his eyes." I glanced across at Darren, who was pretending to drive the burned-out car. "Stupid boys."

"Yeah, bulls are nowhere near as nice as cows, or as useful," said Kate. "Bullocks are thick and bulls are dangerous and unpredictable."

"What's the difference between bullocks and bulls?"

"Bullocks have had their bits cut off."

"Ugh! Why?"

"So that they're easier to manage. Then they're just fed for meat – slaughtered after a couple of years."

I grinned to myself. "Wait till I tell Darren."

"I think we should take 'em back," Kate said.

I checked my watch. "Bit early."

"No. I mean back up to the farm."

"What?"

Before Kate said any more, I heard, "GEMMA!"

Twenty Eight

Darren was pointing towards the gate. Jamie was standing in the road with a bunch of kids from school. There must have been twenty-odd, all looking at the cows. Me and Kate got up and went over.

"What d'you bring *them* for?" Darren asked Jamie as he ran up.

"They wanna help," he replied.

"The whole thing'll be ruined," I said.

"They all knew anyway," said Jamie. He pointed to a boy. "That's Johnny Bracchi – his gran's got one of the cows..." Then he pointed to another. "And that's Chloe Llewellyn."

I recognised the girl that had come to Gran's to see Jane.

"I took one down this morning," said Jamie to the kids. "On a lead like a massive dog." He grinned.

Kate's eyes were narrowed, like she was going to shout.

"D'you still want to take 'em back up to the farm?" I asked.

One of the cows mooed, as if she was saying, "NOOOO!"

Kate looked at the kids. "OK," she said. "We haven't got much time. We'll take 'em out on to the road and you can help take 'em down..." There was a rustle of excitement. "But don't make any sudden moves, and as soon as we get 'em to their owners you all go back to school like nothing happened." They nodded. "If anyone asks, you don't know anything."

Kate, Darren and me guided the cows on to the road and some kids took our bikes. When they saw the cows up close some of them backed away, like they were seeing dinosaurs in the flesh.

We got to the High Street and across the pelican crossing all right, but as we got into the Mawr estate a police car came round the corner and pulled up. The car window slid down. "Where you lot off to with them?" the policeman asked.

"Taking them on to the Mawr Common for a school project," said Kate, cool as you like. "Questions and answers."

"Lot of work for a school project, isn't it? And six cows?"

"Two classes. See, one cow might get nervous with loads of kids around it."

The policeman glanced over to the other policeman. "When I was at school we had to make do with a guinea pig." He looked back at us, but his smile dropped. "Aren't you supposed to inform Defra if you move cows?"

"Only if it's permanent," said Kate. "We'll be taking them back up directly."

"Four stomachs, a cow has," Darren shouted. "Put grass in one end and you get milk out the other – milk for your cornflakes."

"That's put me off my breakfast," said the policeman with a grin. "Get along then. I don't want to hear about any cows on the rampage later. OK?"

"Yes, sir."

The car pulled away. "That was a tight one," Kate said.

I phoned Gran to say we were on the way, and as

we turned into the terrace they were all waiting for us.

"What d'you bring all them for?" said Roger, pointing at the kids.

"They just showed up, Roger. They're here now."

Kate stopped at Morris's first. She gave him the tether. "Morris," she said. "This is Donna."

"She's nervous," he said. "Like me."

"They all are, Morris – new surroundings an' all that."

"Got grass and wild flowers for her."

I noticed his hair blowing in the breeze. He'd washed and he had on clean clothes. "C'mon, girl," he said gently as he led Donna into his backyard.

"C'mon with mine now!" said Roger.

"Rhiannon, this is Roger," Kate said to the cow. "He's a bit loud but he's all right really."

"Cheek." He looked Rhiannon over. "Not as big as Jane, is she?"

"Not all about size," said Gran, watching with her arms crossed. The others came forward to meet their cows.

Peggy was given to Mr Banerjee. He joined his hands and raised them to the sky. "I am blessed."

Maisy was given to Mave Rubens; she was the one who'd been robbed.

"Oh, I'm all jittery," she said. "What if she doesn't take to me?"

"You care for her," said Gran, "and she'll take to you."

"She'll be your guard cow," said Kate.

Mave chuckled.

Cathy was given to Polly.

"Two cats and a cow, I've got now," she said. "Hope they all get on."

The last one, Sophia, went to Tony and Tracey Hughes at the end of the terrace. They were on the dole and they had a little baby.

"Don't expect me to clean up after her, Tone," said Tracey. "I've got enough going on with Candice." The baby was howling, but when she saw the cow she stopped crying and grinned.

That was it. All the cows were delivered to their carers.

"Right, you lot," said Gran to the kids. "I want you to go back to school immediately."

"But, Gran!" said Darren.

"No arguments. We don't want to draw attention to the estate. You can come back after school."

Kate hardly spoke as we went. It's funny, but back in that field she was going to change her mind about the whole thing, and then all the kids turned up. I

realised that even Kate needed back-up. She needed us. Now the cows were on the Bryn Mawr and safe in their new homes. It was mad, really – mad but brilliant.

Twenty Nine

Mam was quiet that evening as we sat at the table. She didn't fuss about me not wanting a chicken Kiev, and gave me an extra dollop of mashed potatoes. Darren was quiet. I was quiet. Mam was quiet.

"Good day at school?" There was something about the way she asked that made me sit up. "Not bad," I said. Darren nodded along with me.

"Funny. Cos the school phoned me asking where you both were. 'Should be there,' I said. 'Well, they're not,' they said..."

I shuddered.

"I remembered how quiet you both were this

morning. Should I call the police? I thought. But then Billy Jones came in for the late shift at work and says, 'Just saw your Gemma taking some cows across the High Street.' Not one cow, but cows plural. So I headed to the Mawr in my break and I spotted you with that Kate girl, and three cows. Little Jamie Thorpe was with you too, so I figured Darren was on duty elsewhere."

I glanced at Darren who was open-mouthed.

"That's right, your mam's a reg'lar Miss Marple. Now tell me, did you really think you could take a load of cows through town without me knowing about it? Because if you did you must be as stupid as you think *I* am!"

She stood up. Furious, she was.

"I said I didn't want your gran getting another pet, you remember? Then the cow turns up and I tell her that I'm not happy, what with the strain and the extra costs and suchlike. But everyone tells me it's fine cos it's a cow and they're useful. Then the next thing you help take another eleven down here. ELEVEN!"

"But they're not all at Gran's, Mam," I said.

"That's beside the point. And you!" she said to Darren. "Gone all cosy with your sister now, haven't you?"

"How d'you mean, cosy?"

I knew exactly what she meant – she was annoyed that Darren was involved.

"Mam, it's not like we brought one here, is it? They're with other people."

"But you didn't tell me, did you? 'Oh Mam, d'you mind if I help take some cows down on to the Mawr estate tomorrow?' No. You did it behind my back. How d'you think that makes me feel? My mam and my own daughter in cahoots!"

"What's cahoots?" asked Darren.

"And the sheer stupidity of it. How long d'you think you can keep eleven cows hushed up?"

"Twelve not eleven," said Darren.

Mam glared at him.

"But they'll be slaughtered."

"Oh, really? And how many cows, d'you reckon, have been killed since you two were born?"

"Loads."

"Loads. Right, and so what makes these ones so special?"

"Mam, they're great," said Darren. "Don't diss 'em. They're massive, useful and good, they are."

"I don't care about cows, Darren. I care about making ends meet, paying bills, getting the food in to feed us, making sure you've got clothes and … and Robbie's back soon ... the useless..." She started

crying. “Fed up, I am!”

Darren grinned. I glared at him. “Sorry, Mam,” I said. “We didn’t do it behind your back on purpose. Just didn’t think.”

I touched her arm.

“D’you realise I’m in every night?” she said. “Three hundred and sixty-five days a year? Every night!”

I’d never thought about it before. It was true.

“You read in the papers about women that leave their young children home alone…” She poked her chest. “I know why they do it, but I haven’t and I wouldn’t.”

“But Mam,” I said. “We could go to Gran’s if you fancied a bingo night.”

“Yeah, ’specially now you’ve got the cow to visit.” She was looking at me with tears in her eyes. “That cow gets more...”

I couldn’t help thinking she was jealous of Jane. Jealous of a cow. She turned and walked into the kitchen, then she spun around. “Tomorrow you’re both in school *all* day. Understood?”

I nodded.

“Promise me now.”

“Promise, Mam,” me and Darren said.

“And any bright ideas you get, like opening a zoo, you ask me first. Right?”

"Right."

She went into the kitchen.

"Mam," said Darren. "If there was a spare cow going..."

"NO!"

I lay in bed that night thinking about everything that had happened. I heard a moo in the distance. Lovely it was, as if I was in the countryside, in the peace and quiet, not on the noisy, ugly Mawr estate. Then another moo came from a different direction. I imagined the cows were talking.

"*It's good here, isn't it?*"

"*Aye, better than that wet and windy field.*"

"*Oh aye, miles better.*"

I went to sleep and dreamed about cows. Running, they were, escaping. All the cows in all the fields all over the country mooing to each other and saying, "*Why should we stay in this field? They'll take our calves, they'll take our milk and then they'll eat us for the trouble.*"

"*Daft, we are.*"

"*S'unfair!*"

"*Yeah, let's go. All we need is grass, nothing else. C'mon!*"

Then they charged off together, strength in

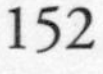

numbers, and burst through wooden gates and hedges. The rebel cows were free. Free to keep their milk for their young and free to live until old age.

"GO GIRLS, GO!"

THIRTY

Everyone knew about the cows at school – no surprise after all the kids helping out.

These girls came up to me during break. I didn't even know who they were. "Going round to Mrs Oleski's at lunch, to see Rachel."

Weird – a girl talking to me about a cow, like it was every day that cows were given out to look after. Then some boys came over – Simon Davis and David Moore – they never usually talk to me. "Gemma, my dad wants to know if there's any chance of a cow?"

"Not at the moment," I said, as if I was some sort of cow merchant.

Apparently, during lunch the canteen was virtually empty and so was the recreation area. The teachers were roaming around asking where the kids had gone.

There was no sign of Kate, and her mobile phone was switched off, so I went to Gran's. I'd never seen the back lane of the terrace so full of people. There were kids in and out of the backyards, asking questions and wanting to feed the cows. At Morris's, the kids stood in a group staring at him as he filled a trough he'd set up for Donna. He'd built a lovely shelter for her too.

"Go'way!" he shouted.

"We just wanna look," a girl said.

"Looking's no good," he replied. "Get her some food!"

The four of them turned and went off like they'd been programmed.

When I got to Gran's she was stood with the kids packed around her, talking to them like a class teacher. "One at a time now," she said. "I don't want her frightened."

"How much she weigh, d'you reckon?" one boy asked.

"Enough to break your toe if she trod on your foot."

"She's not stopped eating."

"Well, she's got a lot of stomachs to fill," said Gran.

"Four!" shouted Darren as he pushed through holding a bin bag. "Look, Gran, fresh grass off the caretaker. Loads more where that came from."

"Kate came by," Gran said to me.

"How was she?"

"Oh, she looked white as snow, Gemma. She's fighting her dad, and I'm worried we've played the wrong hand. I mean, a dozen cows and on the Bryn Mawr of all places."

"Well, they're here now, Gran, and look, everyone's into it and they'll be well cared for. Just think of them sliced up in the butcher's after Mostyn's done with 'em."

"Oh, Gemma!"

"Well, it's true, Gran."

She smiled at me and I knew she was back on track.

"I'll go up to the farm and see her."

"Good idea. Oh, she left a map for you. It's indoors."

I went inside. There was a map on the table – Ordnance Survey. I opened it. It was really big and covered the whole valley. I noticed Kate had drawn circles with little notes where she thought the waterfall might be. She'd done it just for me with

all that was going on with her. The map blurred as my eyes teared up. Gran was suddenly beside me. "What's the map for, Gemma?"

"Nothing important. School."

"Darren told me about your mam – how angry she was," said Gran. "I'll call her later, tell her you're on an errand for me and I'll invite her here for dinner. We'll make peace."

I gave Gran a hug and dashed out.

Before I went up to the farm I wanted to see Karuna, so I went into Mr Banerjee's backyard. His family was there – must have been eight or nine of them. Mr Banerjee saw me and smiled.

"I'll come another time."

"Come, please," he said. "We are celebrating."

Peggy looked lovely. She had a colourful blanket over her and flowers in her hair. "I came to thank your grandson for the flute," I said a bit nervously. "I should have been round before now, but with all that's going on..."

"Karuna is not here," he said. "How is your flute playing?"

"Not much good, to be honest. It's difficult."

"But if you keep practising you'll soon have birds coming to your window to listen." He turned to his family. "This is Gemma, a friend of Karuna."

I liked him saying that. A woman smiled at me, Mr Banerjee's daughter, I reckon. She was stunning-looking. "It is a very generous gift even on a temporary basis."

"Oh yes," I said. "I'll take very good care of it."

She looked confused. "I meant the cow."

"Oh," I said.

"My son told me about you," she said with a smile.

I realised she was Karuna's mam. My cheeks glowed, giving me away. "How's Peggy doing?" I asked.

"Fine," said Mr Banerjee. "She has a good heart and gives me much milk because she is free, like in India."

"I'm on my way to find Kate. I'll tell her Peggy is well settled."

"Don't forget your flute lesson with Karuna."

"I won't." I felt embarrassed and wanted to get away. "Bye."

Thirty One

The farmhouse was closed and there was no one in the milking shed. I wondered where Kate could be. On my way back I passed the field where the cows used to graze. The gate was wide open so I stopped and looked in. It was deserted. I was about to go when I noticed something on the ground.

"Kate!" I shouted.

I let my bike fall and ran. Her parents were probably looking for her, and there she was lying in the cows' field, dead.

Her head snapped up. "What? What's wrong?"

I stood over her, panting. "Nothing's wrong, I just

thought... Are you all right?"

"Yes."

She didn't get up – just lay there, reminding me of the time I lay in the road.

"Haven't seen you," I said. "So I was worried, Gran too." I was desperate to know what her dad and mam had said when they found the cows had gone.

"Thanks for the map. Going to start looking for that place."

I wanted her to ask why I was so keen to find the waterfall, but I guess she had bigger stuff to think about.

"Everyone's got loads of help with the cows," I said. "Gran's giving a butter and cheese-making workshop tomorrow morning. She was saying she was doing a swap with her cheese and butter for straw and grass and such … said it reminds her of the old days. Morris says Donna doesn't give much milk, but he's not bothered. Just likes having her, I reckon."

Kate sat up and gazed across the field, empty of cows. I couldn't wait any more so I sat down beside her. "What did your dad say?"

"He's called Defra – told them the cows are gone."

"Who's Defra?"

"The government department that deals with farming and stuff. You have to tell them when cows

are moved, by law." Kate shook her head. "Stupid."

"Who? Your dad?"

"No!" she said with angry eyes. "Me! Me! This whole thing was stupid. Taking the cows on to the Mawr sorted nothing out. Nothing. My dad's fuming. He'd already gone and put a deposit down on that tree shredder he was talking about."

"So?"

"Think about it! Mostyn's got his field back, but my dad still owes him. All he had to pay him with was the cows – the cows we've got. Mam and Dad can't believe I did it, and nor can I." Her head dropped. I was scared she was going to cry. Kate Thomas, the cowgirl, didn't cry.

A car skidded to a halt, right in front of my bike in the lane. Mr Thomas got out of his truck and walked towards us. "Good fun, is it?"

I got up, but Kate stayed sitting.

"Where are they?"

He was asking *me*. I was terrified.

"What's the point?" he said. "What are you going to solve doing this? When I told Mostyn I had no cows to sell him, he thought I was having a laugh. And the chap at Defra told me to call the police, so I said, 'Well, they haven't exactly been stolen.' 'How d'you mean?' he says. 'Kate, my daughter, took them.'

'Where to?' he asks. 'I don't know,' I says. 'This is very *irregular,*' he tells me. Irregular!" His eyes bulged wide. "What you've done is insane!"

"You didn't try, Dad!"

Kate was standing now and pointing at him. "I understood when the cows were taken to slaughter. I felt sad but I knew it was the way. Then foot-an'-mouth came – 'the plague', you called it – but it was like you caught it instead of the cows. You gave in to Mostyn..."

"Gave in! Those cows are a liability – it's nothing to do with Mostyn."

"You stopped being a farmer, Dad, but I didn't, and I *still* haven't!" Tears were pouring down her face. "Granddad saw this coming."

"When he was alive the herd was already running at a loss," said Mr Thomas just as angrily. "That's what you don't see."

"I don't mean that. I mean you!" she shouted, stabbing a finger at him. "One day he was in the milking shed, talking to Granma about you – they didn't know I was there. He said you didn't have the stomach for farming. He called it right, didn't he? You never had the stomach for it, Dad. But it's not the cows' fault, is it? They've done nothing wrong. Nothing."

She sucked in her breath and sobbed, then she walked off into the field. I realised the cows were all Kate had and now they were gone.

"Where are the cows?" he asked me again.

I was shaking, not because I was scared – I was fuming. I turned and stared him in the eye. "What cows?"

He went back to his truck, looking angry enough to drive over my bike. I ran into the lane and pulled it out the way.

I watched him drive off. He'd have a job going down every street on the estate trying to find the cows, and no one on the Mawr was about to tell him where they were.

Thirty Two

I was late going back, but I got a message from Gran that Mam was on her way to hers for dinner.

It was dark by the time I turned into the alley. I heard a moo and stopped. For a moment I wondered what it was – like I'd forgotten about the cows dotted around the place. I smiled and got off my bike. As I reached Gran's back gate I saw a glint of silver on the ground.

"Karuna!"

He was lying face down and his hand was gripping the flute. I got down and turned him over. His eye was badly swollen and blood was coming out of his

mouth. He smiled. "They didn't get my flute."

I heard footsteps and stood up, braced for trouble.

"Gemma?"

"Mam! He's been beaten up."

She helped me get Karuna to his feet and we took him into Mr Banerjee's backyard. His cow was lying on her bed of straw. She glanced at us nervously.

"It's OK, Peggy," I said.

Mr Banerjee was usually relaxed and smiling, but when he saw the state of Karuna his face went hard.

"We should call the police," Mam said.

"No," said Mr Banerjee. "I call his father and mother first."

"Well, let's clean him up," said Mam. "I wouldn't want to see my boy in this state."

She helped take him inside, then went straight to the kitchen like it was our house. Within a few minutes she was cleaning Karuna's face.

I'd never been inside Mr Banerjee's home. It was so clean. There was a statue of a boy with a blue face playing the flute, and there were paintings of other people with swords and elephant heads, like they were out of a fairy tale.

"Ow!" Karuna winced with pain.

"No broken bones," said Mam.

"Who was it, Karuna?" I asked.

"No idea. They came from behind and grabbed my flute."

He was still holding it tightly. I could see it was scratched and damaged.

"Why do people do this?" said Mr Banerjee. "We are a peace-loving family and would not harm the smallest creature."

"This is not the sort of welcome we want the Bryn Mawr giving newcomers," Mam said. "There *is* no reason for it. It makes me ashamed."

"We can stop it!" I said. It came out a bit loud. "I'm fed up of it, Mam. We can stop it, if we want."

"I'm fed up of it too," she said. "It's not everyone, just a few that don't understand what they do, or even why they do it."

"Your daughter is right," said Mr Banerjee. "We *can* stop it, if we want."

We'd never taken the trouble to get to know Mr Banerjee and yet he's lived next door to Gran for years. He's a lovely man, but it's funny how you can decide you don't like someone for no reason, and then you change – a bit like me and cows.

Karuna brought the flute to his mouth and blew into it. The sound filled the room. It was so clear and bright. I watched the way his lips rested over the hole and his fingers touched the keys. It was lovely, but I

was embarrassed at the same time because I realised I'd been blowing into the wrong hole.

"Sounds OK," he said with a smile. "We could have that lesson tomorrow."

I nodded, but didn't look at Mam.

We made our way to Gran's next door in silence, then Mam said, "Now I know what the hooting noise was." I didn't want to tell her I was blowing in the wrong hole; not that it would have sounded much better if I'd got it right. "Why didn't you tell me he loaned you a flute?" she asked.

"Thought you might laugh."

"Who's laughing? Very nice of him."

I'd expected a sarky remark, I suppose.

All through dinner Mam was quiet, apart from saying that me and Darren should have told her about what we were doing. Gran was upset by what happened to Karuna. It made her sad after all the nice things that were going on with the cows and everything.

That night, when we went to bed, I came out of the bathroom and stopped on the landing. I could just see Mam's legs stretched out as she watched TV downstairs. There was a pile of laundry on the settee beside her. She was on her own.

Dad should be with her, I thought, *keeping her company*.

I felt this flurry of anger rise up in me.

"What you doing?" Darren whispered from his bedroom doorway.

"Nothing."

"Who d'you reckon beat up him next door then?"

He smirked. I went up to him, trying to control my temper.

"Think it's funny do you, Darren?"

He shrugged.

"Shall I tell Gran you think it's funny Karuna got beaten up? *Him* next door!"

The smirk quickly vanished.

"Maybe I'll tell her to ban you from going near any of the cows. I reckon she'll be up for it, an' all."

"All right, sorry."

That was a first for me – Darren apologising. I went into my room and closed the door. I thought of all the times I'd said "*them* next door". And all the things Sian had done in front of me, including calling people horrible names, and I'd said nothing. I was no saint.

There was a knock. "What?"

"Gary Tobin nicked your bike."

I opened the door. Darren backed away. "I didn't

know he was going to do it, Gemma, honest. And when I saw him take it I got scared of what he might do if I grassed on him – nasty, he is."

I realised he was stuck with the bad of the Mawr just like me, but I saw that he was scared too and my anger melted away. "S'all right," I said. "Got it back now."

"*You two!*" yelled Mam from downstairs. "*Go to bed!*"

"Yes, Mam," Darren and me shouted back.

"I'll try and find out who beat up Karuna," he whispered.

I nodded and went back into my room.

Thirty Three

The last of the three circles Kate had drawn on the map was the furthest from the Bryn Mawr. I was getting tired, as I was already about fifteen miles from home. I began to wonder if Dad had taken us further than I'd thought. For all I knew it was a hundred miles away, or over to England, even.

"No," I said out loud. "It was a Welsh waterfall."

I coasted downhill towards the last place marked on the map. I saw a small car park with a sign that said Maes-glas Forest. It was deserted. There was a path that led into some woods. I got off my bike and walked with it.

It was a bit spooky and, to be honest, I was scared, 'specially when I checked my mobile and saw there was no signal. I was miles from home and hadn't told Mam. She would have asked questions about where I was going and might have said, "No. It's silly." I just wanted to get there and see it. The wind was rustling the trees as I walked through the woods, which made it even more creepy. Nothing seemed familiar, but I'd only been that one time, years before. The breeze picked up again, but I heard something else – it was water. There had to be a river or stream nearby otherwise Kate wouldn't have marked it on the map.

I came to a gate but I couldn't get the bike through, so I locked it and carried on.

The path became steep, almost like steps, and the noise of the water got louder. When I got to the bottom I walked under some low branches, and then I saw the waterfall. It was the same one, all right. The one Dad and Darren had stuck their heads under. I was there. It seemed smaller, somehow – I remembered it bigger and louder.

But where was the massive tree and the meadow? As I looked around I realised we'd been there in the summer time – the meadow was completely overgrown. I turned and saw that I'd walked right under the big tree. It had no leaves so I hadn't noticed it.

I put my hand in the water. It was ice cold.

I watched the waterfall tumbling and sloshing, going on forever, and I had the feeling I was in a trance again.

"*Where's the water come from, Mam?*" I heard myself ask back then.

"*Rain,*" she said.

"*But when it stops raining the water would stop.*"

"*It never stops raining in Wales.*"

It seemed impossible to me standing there and watching it pouring down, almost as if it would stop once I'd walked away.

"Mam!" I called out. "MAM! DAD!" I shouted as if I was in trouble.

No answer, except the sound of the water falling and falling. I felt the anger rise up in me. I don't know why – this place wasn't to blame for anything.

I took out the jewellery box and opened it. I gazed around the meadow where me and Darren had explored and Mam and Dad had dozed. It was overgrown. A different place. I tipped out the dried grass and leaves, back from where they came.

I'd come all the way here, but it wasn't the same.

Why did I think it would be?

Thirty Four

The Mawr was different. The cows made it different, according to Gran, and I reckon she was right. Loads of people went round for her butter and cheese classes. People were chatting about the cows everywhere you went. They came to offer hay or grass or a blanket, and in return they'd get fresh milk or some butter or cheese. I noticed that the cows were getting more and more pampered as the days went by: fresh hay was put down so that the ground was soft; they were groomed and cleaned, and the backyards were washed and scrubbed. Morris had even painted a mural of trees and grass on his back wall – said he wanted to give Donna something to look at.

People said their cows had their own personalities: some were restless and some were cool; some mooed a lot, others didn't. Mave's cow was nosy and stuck her head in through the back window, like she wanted to go into the house. I heard Roger make out that his cow, Rhiannon, preferred opera music.

Mam was curious, like everyone else, and went to Gran's to see what was going on. I'm glad she did. She joked about the cows getting more attention than a dozen new babies.

People talked about how bad it was that Karuna was attacked.

"Terrible about Mr Banerjee's grandson. They're evil, people that did that."

"Aye, the dregs of the sewers, they are."

"Scum," said Darren, with a glance at me.

It was like they were wishing away the bad from the Mawr.

One afternoon a reporter was snooping around and asking questions, but all he got was, "Cows? What cows?"

The biggest change was the kids. People like Roger were saying they'd lose interest, but they didn't. They kept going round after school.

I once saw Sian having a go at her brother for

helping Morris out with Donna.

"What's it to you?" Ryan said to her.

"Wait till Mam hears you're helping Mad Morris," she said.

Ryan shrugged. "Tell her. I don't mind. And anyway, he's not mad."

Sian saw me watching. "What you looking at?"

I stared right back. "Nothing," I said to her. "I'm looking at nothing."

She stood there, with Karen, Tracy and Jo, and everything going on around them – kids rushing in and out of the yards and mucking in. They were left out and they weren't used to it. I saw the same look on the faces of the Tobin brothers too. It was like they couldn't take everyone mingling together. That was it – there was no "them and us", it was just everyone.

I realised the Tobins and the Sians all wanted to keep fighting, like they depended on it. They were angry at something and I knew what that was like, but I didn't want to feel it any more.

Thirty Five

Saraswati is the Hindu Goddess of energy and creativity. That's what Karuna told me. Goddess, mind you, not a bloke – well powerful, she is. Interesting how many Gods and Goddesses the Hindus have. Durga was my favourite. She was a slayer of demons, rode on a lion and had ten arms – useful or what?

I found out that the statue in Mr Banerjee's house of the blue boy was Krishna. He's a God and a cow shepherd. All the cow maids fancied him, apparently. Mr Banerjee told me about cows roaming free in the streets in India because they're respected over there. I think Peggy was more than a cow to him; he even

said she was sent to him from God.

Mr Banerjee made us tea and sandwiches while Karuna finally gave me my flute lesson. At first he had me blowing across the top of a bottle, which was embarrassing. Karuna was so patient, like he *wanted* to teach me, which made him even more gorgeous.

"Play me something," I asked.

"What would you like me to play?"

"Anything."

He thought for a moment and talked about this flute music he was studying, by someone called Bark. I nodded as if I knew what he was on about.

He closed his eyes as he played. His head rocked gently but the flute seemed to stay in the same position the whole time, as if his body moved to the flute and not the other way around. I regretted asking him to play, because after about ten seconds I started to cry. I don't mean bawling away, but tears started falling down my cheeks.

That music made me think of everything. It was sad, but warm and cosy too. Everything was squashed into that couple of minutes of him playing. I thought how different me and Karuna were, like we were from different planets. As soon as he finished I stood up. "I got to go."

"Are you all right?"

I nodded. "Thank you," I said. "That was..." The only word I could think of was a word I couldn't ever remember saying. "That was beautiful."

Mr Banerjee smiled at me, like he understood.

When I was outside I rubbed my cheeks dry, and breathed deeply. I could smell cow poo, but it's not a bad smell – it just smells of countryside.

Peggy eyeballed me. I touched her and realised again how soft cows feel, like velvet. I stroked her and stroked her.

Who could be scared of cows? They're beautiful.

I felt good, like everything was going to be all right. Then Morris went and took Donna on to the Common.

THIRTY SIX

By the time I got down to the Common there was a small crowd around Morris, who had Donna on a tether. My heart was banging in my chest, as I was expecting the police to show up any second.

"What you doing, Morris?"

"Getting frustrated, she was," he said. "Needed a walk. Loads of fresh grass here doing nothing."

"Is this one of the Bryn Mawr dozen?" a woman in the crowd asked.

"Aye, that's right," said Morris. "Done her a power of good, this did. Maybe she misses being with the others too, don't you think?"

"Maybe," I said. "But let's get her back now, Morris."

Everyone was looking grim at Gran's house. Kate had come down, and there was Mr Banerjee, Roger, Polly and a few others.

"It might only be a matter of time now before they're found," said Gran.

"Bloody Morris!" muttered Roger. "I'm going to give him a piece of my mind."

"You'll do no such thing," snapped Gran. "He was thinking about Donna. Those cows are doing us a service, and we owe them a lot. It's been lovely having Jane, but I've been guilty of thinking of myself." She looked at Kate. "You say the word and they can all go back up to that field of theirs."

"Oh Lil, no!" said Mave. "My Maisy's settled in lovely now."

Everyone started chipping in.

"They're not ours to decide," shouted Gran. "Those cows belong to Kate and Mr Thomas, and if the best thing for them is to take 'em back, then that's what we'll do."

"No, Gran!"

Darren ran in from the backyard. "Don't give 'em back, please. They'll be killed."

That did it for me – the last time I saw Darren that upset it was because Mam had banned him from his video games for an evening.

"Shush now, Darren," said Gran. "I've been pleased as punch the way you've taken to that cow – you've been a different boy – but this can't go on forever."

"Why don't you speak to that reporter, Gran?" I said. "The one that was hanging around."

"Why?"

"Well, maybe it would help if more people knew about the cows ... 'specially if they knew they'd be killed?"

"I don't know, Gemma. It might rub people up the wrong way. Shall I have a word with your father, Kate?"

She shook her head. "He's too angry," she said. "He's not even talking to me at the moment. Besides, the cows are here now. We won't do them any favours moving them again."

"But they're still yours, Kate," said Gran. "We haven't forgotten that."

We went out into the alley. Me and Kate stood watching everyone going in and out of the backyards. She looked lost.

"D'you want to borrow my bike to get back up?" I asked.

"No."

"It'll take you ages to get home."

"No!" she snapped.

I was going to snap back, but as I watched her plod off up the alley I realised we had her cows and she was just left with a bad atmosphere at home. I wanted to help her and then I remembered what that woman had called the cows.

"The Bryn Mawr dozen," I said out loud.

It was like they were famous.

Thirty Seven

We were on the train to see Dad and all I could think about were the cows.

I usually liked the train journey but I didn't want to be away from the Mawr, and that was a first. Mam had the *South Wales Echo* spread on the table because there was an article about the cows. She read it to us – "The Mystery of the Bryn Mawr Dozen", it was called.

"*'The cows have made a big difference to the Mawr since they arrived,' the anonymous caller claimed. 'And people love them.' No one would say where the cows are, but Local Councillor Rhys Morgan admitted, 'Things are strangely quiet on the Bryn Mawr. The police informed me that domestic incidents are down and we've had no burglaries in a while. I've not seen any cows, mind you, though I have heard the odd moo late at night...'*"

Mam shook her head. "Your gran's upset about this. She reckons it was probably Roger who told them, but he swears he didn't."

I felt myself blush and hoped Mam didn't notice.

"Think the cows'll still be there when we get back?" Darren asked me.

"Yeah," I said, but I wasn't sure.

I was feeling funny on that train, all tense like, but it wasn't just the cows.

When Mam took out sandwiches she'd made for the journey I was worried they'd all be meat. I didn't want an argument, 'specially the way I was feeling. She handed me a foil-wrapped sandwich and said, "I did you cheese and tomato, as you're a veggie now."

Surprised, I was. "Thanks."

I gazed out the window and saw cows in the fields. The first time I'd gone to see Dad I wouldn't have given a thought to them; but here I was, me, Gemma Matthews, looking out for cows like they were lions on a safari.

When we arrived we had to go into the waiting

room, which was always full of other relatives and friends waiting to see whoever was inside. I've never got used to it. I've always felt like we were all being punished, and I didn't want to be there, not now. Then they started calling out names and we went through.

Dad was grinning at us as we entered. We each hugged him and sat down. Mam showed him the newspaper article. He laughed. "The Mawr never ceases to amaze me," he said. "Your gran ought to sell her cow while she's got the chance."

"How d'you mean?" I asked.

"Well, I bet she could find someone to take it off her hands," said Dad. "Worth a few bob, I reckon."

"No, Dad," said Darren. "Fantastic, it is."

"I don't think she'd sell it for a million, Rob," said Mam. "She's really taken to it, and her neighbours – some of them have got one an' all."

"Oh aye," said Dad, but he wasn't interested.

Mam started talking about this and that, then she went on about a big gas bill she'd had to pay.

Dad nodded. "That's a lot, isn't it?"

"It is, Robbie. You're telling me it's a lot," said Mam. "We gotta keep warm."

"Course you have – never said you shouldn't." He glanced at me. "What's the matter with you?"

"Nothing," I said, but I was feeling funny, kind of shaky.

"Gemma's learning to play the flute," said Mam.

"What for?"

"To play it, Robbie," she said. "Why else would you learn an instrument? She's getting lessons off Mr Banerjee's grandson – he loaned her the flute."

"Banerjee?" said Dad.

"Aye," said Mam. "Nice of him, I thought."

"How old is this boy then?"

I didn't like him asking that. The trembly feeling got worse.

"Fourteen, fifteen," said Mam.

"Should she be going round on her own?" he asked her, as if I wasn't there.

"It's fine, Robbie," she said. "They're all right."

I could really feel myself getting wound up.

"Gran's making cheese now, Dad," said Darren.

"And butter," said Mam. "You ought to see her."

He nodded. "I'm not happy about Gemma going next door on her own."

"You can't stop me, Dad."

I said it loud and people looked round.

"What did you say?"

"Mam can stop me, sure, but you can't because you're in here."

He was shocked. "Gemma, don't talk to me like that."

I didn't care he was annoyed – in fact, it pleased me. "What are you doing here?" I said.

"What?"

"I don't know anyone in school whose dad's in prison. My bike was nicked the other day and Kate got it back for me. Not you, Kate did."

"Who's Kate?"

"Doesn't matter!" I stood up. "Someone nicked my bike, but I couldn't ask you to help because you're in here." His eyes went wide. "You're missing it all, Dad. The Mawr's different now, but you wouldn't know because you're in here. You get food and you're kept warm. Mam's working. She's paying the bills. She's getting the food in. She's doing what mams do, but *you*...!"

I pointed at him, my hand shaking. I was so angry – angry at him being in prison; angry that Mam was always wound up and on her own every night; angry that cows have a short life; and angry because the waterfall wasn't the same. Angry, angry, angry.

"Gran called you useless," I said. "And she's right – while you're in here you're as useless as a teat on a bull!"

I walked out.

❋❋❋

I fell asleep on the journey back, and dreamed about cows roaming free in India, like Mr Banerjee had told me. When I woke I looked at Mam and she smiled. I couldn't remember the last time I saw her smile at me. Darren was quiet, just gazing out the window. Then Mam got a text message. "I don't believe it," she said when she read it.

"What is it?" me and Darren asked. "Is it the cows?"

She nodded.

"Ah, no," said Darren. "Are they gone?"

"No," said Mam. "Your gran ... she says they're on the telly!"

Thirty Eight

We huddled round the TV at Gran's house. She'd already seen it earlier, but we had to wait for the BBC Wales news at six o'clock.

I couldn't believe my eyes when it came on.

A reporter was walking across the Mawr Common.

"*The Bryn Mawr estate is often in the news for all the wrong reasons,*" he said. "*Ask anyone on this estate and they'll tell you about petty crime, burglary, joyriders, graffiti and intimidation. One elderly lady I spoke to said she was too frightened to leave her house alone. But recently a change has come about on this estate – it's quiet, the crime rate is down and, if rumour is to be believed, that change has been brought about by an animal. Not a cat or a dog, but a cow, a dairy cow.*"

He walked up to an alley doorway on the terrace. Children were surrounding him. "There's Jamie!" Darren shouted.

The reporter entered one of the backyards and there was the cow.

"*No one would tell me where this cow came from,*" he said. "*And what's all the more surprising is that it's not the only one; I'm told there is a round dairy dozen. Twelve cows dispersed on the Bryn Mawr, and homes found for each one of them. One of these cow-carers was prepared to talk to me, but he didn't want to appear on camera.*"

"*I love that cow,*" said the carer. Even with his back to the camera I could tell it was Roger. "*She asks for nothing, other than grass. And I don't know what it is, but I just feel calm when I'm with her. Know what I mean?*"

"*Where's the cow from?*" the reporter asked.

"*I can't say, but I can't give her back. Not now. We've bonded, see.*"

"*Did you know that a dozen cows have been reported missing from the farm of Nigel Thomas?*"

"*All I know is that this cow is happy, well fed and giving milk freely. There's years of life left in*

her. I mean, where would you prefer to be – alive and well cared for, or hanging up on a butcher's hook?"

The reporter was standing beside the cow again. "*Earlier today I spoke to Ron James, a milkman on the Bryn Mawr.*"

"*In the last week trade has definitely dropped off,*" said the milkman. "*Now if it's because of these cows I've heard about, well, ironic isn't it? I got nothing against cows – I'm a milkman – but they should be on a farm, not in the middle of town.*"

The reporter was back on the Mawr Common. "*We tried to speak to Nigel Thomas, the owner of the missing cows, but he declined to be interviewed. The mystery of the so-called 'Bryn Mawr Dozen' remains unresolved. One thing is for sure, this estate is not the same and this story is not over.*"

The news report finished and I felt terrible. Gran, Mam and Darren were grinning, but I had this sinking feeling – I realised it wasn't a game, it was serious.

"D'you know now who contacted the paper?" Mam asked Gran.

"No. But whoever it was did us a favour, I think."

"No, they didn't," I said.

"Why?" Gran asked.

I took a deep breath. "It was me who phoned the paper."

"You!"

"Yeah, and I wish I hadn't. It was stupid. I just thought that if more people got to know about the cows it would help somehow. But now they've been on the telly it's gone too far. So we should get them all out in the open, like Morris did."

"Why?" asked Gran.

"Well, Mr Thomas will have seen the news. He's not thick. He'll come and round them up, most like. Our only chance is that when he sees how much everyone loves the cows, maybe he'll change his mind."

"Can't we just move them to a different house every night?" suggested Darren. "They'll never find 'em."

"The cows wouldn't thank us for that, love," said Gran. "No, your sister's right. What's the point of hiding them now?" She sighed. "We should make the first move and get them out."

"And we should tell Mr Thomas," I said.

"Yes," agreed Gran. "They are his."

"And Defra," I added.

Gran nodded. "I'll phone Mr Thomas now."

"Let me go tell him tonight," I said. "Be straight with him."

"We can phone," said Mam. "It's late."

"I want to go up there face-to-face, and I want to see Kate too."

"Go on then, but I want you straight back."

"Right," said Gran. "I'll do some calling around. Let's just hope it works."

Thirty Nine

When I knocked on the farmhouse door I could hear my heart beating through my open mouth. The door opened and Mr Thomas was staring down at me.

"Brought the cows, have you?"

I waited for him to let me in, but he didn't.

"Nigel," I heard Kerry say, behind him.

Mr Thomas pushed open the door. I stepped inside and there was Kerry standing by Kate, who was sitting at the table. The three of them waited for me to speak.

"We're..." My voice was almost a whisper. "We're taking all the cows on to the Mawr Common

tomorrow morning. We're not hiding them any more."

"Not much point after showing them on the telly, is there? Have you told Defra?"

"My gran's calling them now."

"This is not the end of it, you know?" said Mr Thomas. "I'm going to prosecute for lost earnings."

I glanced at Kate, but she was looking down at the table.

"Shall I tell you the irony? And you can tell this to everyone that's stolen one of my cows," said Mr Thomas. "Mostyn doesn't want them any more. Now this saga's been in the papers and on the telly he doesn't want them. He wants his money, of course, but not the cows. There's no other dairy farmer round here, so the quickest way I can pay him back is to take them straight to slaughter. And you all thought you were saving them."

"It was a crazy thing to do, love," said Kerry. "It's only made things worse."

I could feel my confidence dribbling away. "Well," I said. "The cows will be on the Common tomorrow morning, waiting."

"Good. You can help Kate bring 'em all back up here."

I looked at the small, sad Kate with her head

bowed. I wanted to say something, anything, but I just felt like a stupid little girl.

Outside I climbed on to my bike, but as I pushed off my legs had no strength to pedal. All I could think about was what Gran and everyone else on the Mawr would think when I told them that Jane, Donna, and the rest of the Bryn Mawr Dozen were going to slaughter.

I stopped at the top of the hill and gazed down on the twinkling lights of the Mawr estate. It seemed like a toy town, unreal. As I started down the hill I had another idea, which was also probably stupid, but now I was past caring.

I swerved off the hill, and stopped at the entrance to Mostyn's farm – huge place it was.

I started cycling along the drive, but before I got near the farmhouse a big black car came towards me. The driver was squashed behind the wheel, even though the car was the size of a bus. He brought it to a halt and the window near to me opened with a hiss.

"You lost?" he asked.

"Are you Mr Mostyn?"

"I am."

He had a big belly and his face was red, like he was about to shout.

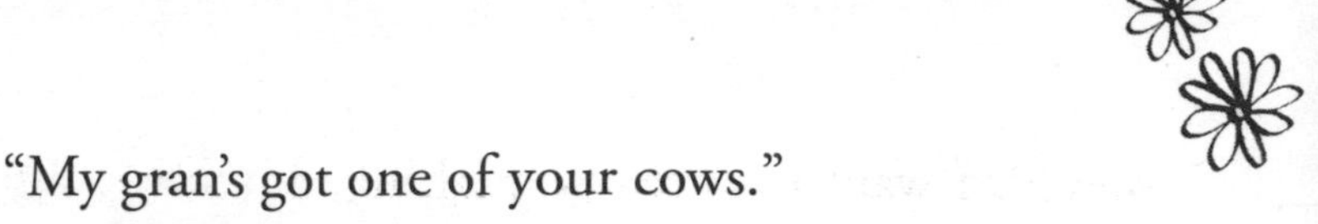

"My gran's got one of your cows."

His forehead crinkled. "You mean your gran *stole* one of Nigel Thomas's cows. They're not mine."

"The cow was Kate's to give."

"What d'you want?"

I gripped the handlebars, fighting my nerves.

"Why don't you give us the cows?"

"Huh? They're *not* mine! Ask Thomas to give away his cows."

"He can't. He needs the money to pay you."

Mostyn nodded. "That's right. I've got my field back. Now I want my money. And what gives you the idea *I'm* in a position to give away cows?"

"You're a big-time farmer. You got money."

He laughed. His teeth were yellow and horrible. "That it? Flattery?" He jabbed his fat finger at me. "Listen. Thomas was handed down his farm on a plate – I started mine from scratch! So you go back down the Mawr and tell them to give Thomas back his cows, then he can honour his debt – the debt he owes *me*."

"Please, Mr Mostyn," I said. "I told the papers and now I feel really bad. Please save 'em!"

"Kate Thomas was round here asking me the same thing. So I'll tell you what I told her – I don't *want* them now, girly. I want my *money*."

I didn't like him calling me girly. Money, money, money – that's all he cared about. So for the second time today I lost it.

"It's all your fault!"

"What?"

"You put Mr Thomas under pressure," I said, jabbing a finger back at him. "Kate was only trying to save the cows. She cares, is all. If you were a cow you'd be well dead and eaten by now. My gran *needs* that cow and so does everyone else. You don't, you got loads. You don't live on the Mawr. You don't know what it's like. You haven't got a clue. 'Miser Mostyn' they call you – no wonder!"

I turned my bike around and cycled away. Mr Thomas didn't care, Mostyn just wanted money, and Dad was inside and no help. Useless, the lot.

I screamed all the way down the hill.

FORTY

As soon as I got in they asked me how it went.

"Fine," I said. "He was angry, of course."

I didn't want to tell them Kate's dad had said he'd take them straight to be killed, 'specially as I saw Gran and Darren looking so hopeful. They told me everyone had agreed taking them on to the Common was a good plan, apart from Roger. I realised that this time tomorrow all the cows might be on their way to the slaughterhouse, and all because of my big mouth.

That night I sat at the top of the stairs and listened to Mam talking on the phone. "Well, she takes after me, Robbie ... says it how it is... You should've called earlier – she's in bed now... Scared, are you? It's strange, Rob, but things are different round here. Everyone says it's because of the cows. I don't know. All I can say is that it's different..."

When she hung up I watched her. She took out a cigarette and put it in her mouth. She picked up her lighter, then she stopped, sighed and pulled the cigarette out. Her head dropped back against the settee.

I went quietly downstairs.

"What are you doing out of bed?" she asked.

"Thirsty, Mam – really thirsty." I went into the kitchen. "Want some water?"

"No."

I filled and emptied a glass a few times, then I took a sip and went to the doorway of the lounge. Mam was staring at nothing. I walked to the settee and sat beside her. My heart was pounding. I thought she might tell me to go back upstairs, but I wanted to be with her. I sipped at the water and Mam didn't say anything. We both just sat there staring at the TV that was off. I remembered sitting on that settee snuggled up to her. It was so long ago it felt like a dream.

"That was your dad on the phone," she said.

"Oh, yeah," I said as cool as I could. "What did he want?"

"I think he was a bit shook up by you having a go at him."

"Just saying how it is," I said.

Mam looked at me. "Did him good to hear it, 'specially coming from you. I know he's all grins when we visit and you'd think he was in a holiday camp, but he wants to be out. He ended up inside because he's gullible, Gemma. People took advantage of him. I know that now."

I nodded. I wanted to keep her talking.

"Do I look angry, Mam?"

"Angry?"

"Yeah, have I got an angry sort of face?"

Like Sian, I thought.

"No. Not at all. You've got a pretty face."

I felt all hot suddenly. My throat went dry so I took another sip of water.

"What d'you do, Mam? In your job, like?"

"How d'you mean?"

"I just want to know what you do, cos I don't know."

"Well, there's not a lot to say. It's an electronics factory and I'm at the most boring end – sticking the parts in boxes as they come through."

"And what do the parts do?"

Mam thought for a moment. "D'you know what?" she said. "I haven't a clue. I can't believe it. I've been working there a couple of years now and I haven't a clue!" She shook her head and laughed.

"Why don't you ask to do something else?"

"Shoving things in boxes is about my level, Gem," she said. "That's why I nag you about school and homework, because, I tell you, you don't want a job like mine when you leave school – rots your brain. There are days when I feel like a robot."

"What were you doing before?"

"Dole mostly, when I first left school. Then I had a job in the canteen at a car factory where I met your dad. I enjoyed that. I liked spreading the mash over the shepherd's pie."

"What happened?"

"You happened."

"Sorry," I said.

Mam's forehead crinkled up. "I didn't enjoy it that much, Gemma. I was happy to be pregnant."

"I bet you could do something else, Mam."

"What's all this about?"

"Nothing, Mam. Just don't like the thought of you not liking your job."

She looked at me funny, like she was trying to suss

me out. "Can't be too choosy round here, Gemma."

"D'you think it'll help, Mam – taking the cows on to the Common, I mean?"

"I've no idea, love, if I'm honest."

We sat there for a while, then she chuckled.

"What?"

"Just remembered what you said to your dad... 'Useless as a teat on a bull'."

She started laughing, and that got me going. We laughed together and then we listened to the silence.

"C'mon now, love. Off to bed."

"OK." I took the glass back to the sink. When I turned she was still sat staring at the switched-off TV, on her own. I went back, and as I passed her I bent down and kissed her on the cheek.

"Love you, Mam."

I ran upstairs and closed the door to my room. My heart was in my mouth. I got into bed and lay there in the dark, listening. I tried to remember if anyone apart from Mam had ever called me pretty, but I couldn't.

Forty One

I was up way too early the next day. I felt like electricity was running through me, I was so nervous. Darren was quiet at breakfast, and Mam seemed even more jittery than me.

"Mam, what's up?"

"I suppose I should have said something last night, but it's your dad..."

Darren stopped eating.

"He's coming home next weekend."

"You never said."

"Yeah, well, there's been so much going on. 'Reintegration leave', it's called, and it's just for

the weekend."

Darren grinned, but I felt well annoyed – the timing was crap. Mam must have noticed, because she said, "I want us all to have an easy time, Gemma. We got enough on our plates as it is, so let's just make the most of it, please."

"OK, Mam."

By the time we got to the terrace everyone was out of their backyards with their cows. Gran was fussing from the off. She got Darren, Ryan and Jamie to take a table over to the Common, as she wanted to offer her cheese and butter to people. Then everyone was standing and waiting in silence.

"Oh, let's go before I burst," Gran said.

"You sure now, girl?" Roger asked.

"We've phoned Defra," said Gran. "We've told them what we're doing and I'm true to my word. *Que sera, sera*, as Doris Day said. So away we go."

We led the cows down towards the Common. Mam walked alongside Gran with Jane. I went with Karuna, Mr Banerjee and Peggy, and Darren walked with Morris and Donna. It was so tense.

When we got to the end of the alley and I saw the Common I was shocked – there were loads and loads of people there. Some held up boards saying

"Save the Bryn Mawr Dozen". At the far end of the Common the other cows were being led on to the grass by their carers.

"Amazing," Karuna said.

The Bryn Mawr Dozen were out in the open, and the TV cameras were there to see it. Gran turned to me with a big grin. "It's like the times we had fetes here, Gemma."

As soon as the cows got on to the grass they started chomping away and the people stood in a huge circle, as if they were protecting them. For a while we just watched the cows eating. They tugged and chewed at grass like they were in competition with each other. All you could hear was their munching and snorting.

Slowly, people drifted about meeting the cows and talking to their carers. It wasn't long before a police van arrived, lights flashing. About five or six policemen stepped out and looked around. I don't think they knew what to make of it.

People were packed around Gran's cheese-tasting table and stuffing themselves. "Lovely," a woman said as she ate. I recognised her as one of the ladies at the crossing when we'd brought the cows down.

"So what's happening with these beauties, Lilly?" she asked.

"We don't know yet, Lorna," said Gran. "Mr Thomas has been told they're here. We're expecting him any moment and we're just hoping for the very best."

"It's nice having them around," she said. "Sort of calming effect they have, don't they?"

"It's like I've always had her," said Gran, stroking Jane. "She's got a gentle temperament. If I could have her in the lounge of an evening I would. And look what she gives us." She waved at the cheese and butter on the table.

Lorna nodded. "Aye. Here, take this." She offered Gran some money.

"Oh, I'm just sharing the cheese, Lorna," said Gran. "Not selling it."

"And I'm not buying," she replied. "It's for the cows."

She put two pounds on the table and went. The coins looked like gold, twinkling in the sunlight. I glanced at Gran just as the TV reporter came up to her.

"D'you own this cow, madam?" he asked.

"No, dear. She's God's own cow."

"No. What I meant was—"

"Here, try some of this." Gran shoved some cheese at the reporter and stopped him in his tracks.

Then I heard a loud click and a voice said, "*Can I have your attention, please...*" It was a policeman holding a megaphone. "*These cows are not allowed on this public ground...*"

Standing next to the policeman were Mr Thomas and Kate. Somehow she seemed smaller, as if she'd turned into Kate's imaginary younger sister. She gazed at all the people, and when she spotted me I felt my insides turn. I wondered what she was thinking of us all.

"*They were moved from their farm without the correct notification. So by order of the Department of Environment they have to be inspected,*" said the policeman. "*We don't want any fuss, just let the Defra inspector do his job and check them over.*"

The man from Defra was wearing wellies and had a clipboard. He turned to Kate's dad. "Are they yours?"

Mr Thomas nodded.

The nearest cow to the inspector was Donna. She seemed nervous, and I can't blame her. "Looking after her, I am," Morris said to the Defra man. "She's fine."

"I need to inspect this cow," he said, but Morris stood in his way.

"Don't take her off me," he pleaded.

Gran called to him and Morris reluctantly shuffled

aside. The Defra man checked the tag on the cow's ear and ticked his clipboard.

"What have you been feeding her?" he asked Morris.

"Hay and grass. Took her here the other day to stretch her legs and have a feed."

The Defra man touched Donna's udders. She mooed. "Seems fine," he said.

"That's what I told you," said Morris.

We watched in silence as the Defra man inspected the rest of the cows. The carers glared at him as he went from one to the next. Finally, he went up to Mr Thomas and had a word with him.

"Here we go," said Gran. "The moment of truth."

Mr Thomas went over to the policeman and was given the megaphone.

"*These cows were taken from my farm without permission...*" His voice echoed around the Common. "*You all knew that when you took them in. The police say I could press charges...*"

Murmurs came from the crowd.

"*No harm seems to have come to them, but you took them, you can bring them back. So here's the deal. If they're all up at my farm by the end of today, I won't take matters any further.*"

He handed the megaphone back to the policeman.

As he walked away, the crowd parted. The shrunken version of Kate was left standing by herself, and all you could hear were the cows pulling and chewing at the grass.

Forty Two

People spoke in whispers as I walked towards Kate. I didn't know what she was going to say – maybe she'd be angry and blame me. She gazed around as if she was wondering why there were so many people on the Common.

"Sorry, Kate," I said. "This was all my idea, and it was me who told the papers."

"Was it?" she said sadly. "Glad it's over and finished with, to be honest."

"Did he mean it last night about the cows going to slaughter?" I asked her.

"I don't know. He has to find a new buyer, or take

them to market, and that means more time and money."

Gran came over to us, with Mam, who had her arm around Darren. "I'm so sorry, Kate," she said. "It just goes to show you can make bad decisions even at my time of life."

"It's OK, Lilly," said Kate. "I started it all off."

The cow-carers gathered around us. They were all so sad.

"C'mon," said Gran. "No point delaying the inevitable. Enough damage has been done. Let's get these cows back up Craig-y-Nos."

"I don't want to give her back," Morris said as he stroked Donna.

"Nor do any of us," said Gran. "We got carried away, taking those cows, but what we did was plain wrong and now we have to face the consequences. It was lovely having them all on the Common, and me giving out the cheese reminded me of the fetes we used to have here." She turned to Kate. "You going to take them all up in one go?"

"No. Six at a time, like we took them down."

"Take Jane up in the first lot, would you?" said Gran.

Jane looked up from her chewing as if she'd heard. Gran walked up to her. "I've got to say goodbye to you, Jane, my beauty. Thanks for your milk, and thanks for keeping me company too."

Gran kissed her on the head. I had to hold my breath to stop myself bursting into tears.

"Stay with her, Lilly," said Kate. "We'll take her second time around. She was first down, let her be the last up."

Gran smiled.

We herded six cows together, and then me, Kate and Darren started on our way. The people that had cared for the cows began to follow us.

Kate turned to them. "S'all right, we can manage."

"We want to come, love," said Maria Bracchi. "We've got nothing else to do."

People watched us taking the six cows across the High Street and on towards Craig-y-Nos hill. It was sad, like a funeral procession. Cars stopped and waited for us to pass. As we got near to the motorway bridge Gran called on my mobile.

"What's up, Gran?"

"*It's Donna – something's wrong.*"

"How d'you mean?"

"*I don't rightly know.*"

I could hear Donna mooing in the background, but she didn't usually make much noise. I passed the phone to Kate. She listened to Gran, then said, "OK.

I'll be there soon." She turned to us. "I need to go back."

"What about the cows?"

"Take them into the field by the bridge, for now. Darren, you know where."

He nodded.

"I won't be long," said Kate. "Probably something and nothing."

I went with her, but her usual slow, plodding walk soon turned into fast strides.

FORTY THREE

When Donna mooed it wasn't the usual sort of moo, it was more like a groan.

They'd taken her back to Morris's yard. Kate ran her hand over Donna's belly and she walked all around her.

"What is it?" I asked.

"She's too early, but I think she's ready to calve."

Gran brought her hand to her mouth. "Oh, love."

"But something's not right." For the first time I saw fear in Kate's eyes. She looked at me and said, "I need my dad."

When Kate phoned him her voice was small and she sounded scared. I thought Mr Thomas would refuse to come, but she hung up and said, "He's on his way."

It was getting dark, and news soon got around that Donna was going to calve. Morris had his kitchen lights on but it wasn't enough, so people brought lamps and gathered in the yard. There was a warm glow of light, which reminded me of a picture of the Nativity I saw once.

Every time Donna let out a moo we all felt for her. It was awful, so Karuna played the flute to calm us. When we heard Mr Thomas's truck coming down the alley the tension got worse. The car door slammed shut and the crowd parted to let Mr Thomas into the yard. He stood there for a moment, staring at us. Here we all were, standing around Donna, a cow we'd taken from him, who was now in trouble. She let out a groaning moo as if she was saying, "Get a move on!"

"Thank you for coming," said Gran.

Mr Thomas looked over Donna. She mooed. "Easy, girl." He went to the truck and came back with a long plastic thing. He handed it to Kate.

"Dad, I—"

"They're your cows," he said. "Get cleaned up and find out what's wrong." He turned to us. "We'll need

more straw."

Some of the neighbours went off as soon as he said that. Mr Thomas went to his truck and returned with a can of something that he sprayed on Donna's behind – disinfectant, Gran said it was. When Kate came out she was wearing the long plastic glove that went right up to her shoulder. She went to the back of Donna.

"Reach in as far as you can," her dad said, "and tell me what you feel."

Donna snorted as Kate slid her arm in. I breathed in sharply. After a few moments she said, "I can feel a foot."

"Can you feel the calf's head?"

"No."

"OK, try and pull the foot round. Don't worry about hurting her – it'll only make it easier."

I could see Kate grit her teeth as she pulled. Donna mooed.

"I've shifted it a bit."

"Now try again to feel for the head, or the nose of the calf."

Kate grunted as she reached in. "There's something... Yeah, it's the head."

I was so tense. Mr Banerjee was praying. I glanced at Karuna, who smiled and made me feel everything would be OK.

"Now you've got to try and bring the head round and reach the other leg."

Kate pulled back a little and Donna cried out. Morris tried to soothe her.

"OK, the head's facing forward."

"Now go as far as you can," said Mr Thomas. "Try and find the right shoulder. Then you can pull the leg round."

Kate reached in and Donna mooed loudly.

"I can't."

"You can."

"Take over, Dad!"

"No. Try again."

Kate winced as she stretched. Donna mooed and Gran moaned along with her. Mam put her arm round me and I held her hand.

Kate gasped. "Got the knee."

"Good. Straighten it and pull her round."

Kate clenched her jaw. Donna staggered, which made Kate slip.

"Easy, girl," said Mr Thomas.

Now Kate was standing on tiptoe and her legs trembled.

Donna started mooing continuously.

"Make sure the head is not tipping back," said Mr

Thomas. "It should be between both hooves."

Kate's expression was determined. Her face was red with the effort as she pulled. Then her hand came out holding two little hooves.

"She'll take over, Kate," her dad said. "Let her go."

Kate stood back. Donna snorted. Then I saw the nose – the nose of a baby cow – and I couldn't stop myself crying. With another push from Donna, the calf's head hung down limply. I put my arm round Darren, who was in tears too. Then, with a final push, the calf dropped on to the bed of straw.

"Good girl!" said Morris proudly.

I blew air out my cheeks.

Donna's calf was covered in blood and slime. Mr Thomas got down and started massaging it – it wasn't breathing.

Kate knelt beside him. Without being asked she lifted the calf's head, forced open the mouth and blew into it. Nothing.

She tried again and I saw the calf's belly expand.

There was a snort and the calf cried out, sounding more like a baby lamb.

We all watched in silence as she struggled to get up. We willed her to stand on her own legs. She was so delicate – her legs looked like they could snap in half. She stumbled, and tried to get up again and again. She wobbled, staggered and fell. When she finally stood up she took two steps, raised her head and started taking milk from Donna. There were "ooh"s and "aah"s from all of us as Donna began to lick her clean. Everyone had tears in their eyes, even Roger.

"Thanks, Dad," said Kate. "I couldn't have done it without you."

Mr Thomas seemed uncomfortable, like he'd forgotten we were there.

FORTY FOUR

As we waited for Kate to clean herself up Mr Thomas stood in Gran's kitchen with his arms tightly wrapped around his chest.

"What about the calf?" Gran asked as she made tea. "I mean, what do we need to do?"

"Donna will look after her," he said. "She's done it before. But she'll need some fodder, so I'll drop some by tomorrow."

"But ... don't you want them up at the farm?"

"Not the best time to be moving a cow and her calf. Better they stay here for now. That doesn't mean all the cows," he added sternly. "Just the cow and newborn."

There was a knock on the door. I opened it to Kerry. She walked in just as Kate came down the stairs. "Everything all right?" she asked.

"She did fine," said Mr Thomas.

"Yeah, Donna was great," Kate said. "So patient."

"I meant you," said her dad. "Proud of you, I was."

Kate's face suddenly crumpled up. "Sorry, Dad. I'm sorry. I made such a mess of things. I don't know why..."

Kerry hugged her. I felt like me and Gran shouldn't have been there, like we were in *their* kitchen looking on.

Mr Thomas sat down at the table with a sigh. "Oh, it was already a mess, Kate. Your granddad was right, I don't have the stomach for farming. I should have done something about it long ago."

"He did say that, Dad," said Kate. "But that's not all..."

"What he said was nothing I didn't already know."

"No. He also said to Granma that you could bend wood with your hands, and that you had green fingers. Said you'd make a fine carpenter or gardener."

"Wish he'd said it to me," Mr Thomas muttered.

"I told it to you wrong, on purpose," said Kate. "I was mad at you."

"I sometimes wish I was a proper farmer like Mostyn," he said. "Driving to be bigger and better."

"I don't," said Kate.

"Me neither," said Kerry.

"I tell you what was peculiar," said Mr Thomas. "Seeing those cows on the Mawr Common. It triggered a memory – me taking cows down there as a boy, with my dad. Then they built the Mawr estate and it wasn't safe to bring them down there any more."

"The cows!" said Kate. "I forgot. We took six up to the field by the motorway."

"They brought them back," said Gran. "When they realised Donna was going to calve they decided they couldn't leave them overnight. Sorry, Mr Thomas, we'll take them all up to you tomorrow."

"Well, nothing's changed," he said. "I still need to sell those twelve cows."

"Thirteen now," said Gran.

He nodded. "Aye, thirteen. I could take them to the livestock market, but just the cost of taking them there isn't going to help me... I could go see Mostyn, cap in hand, ask him to reconsider; though he was pretty annoyed with me, as you can imagine."

I thought of my meeting with Mostyn – I'd probably blown any chance of him changing his mind.

"How much would we need to buy them?" Gran asked.

"Oh, a lot. Thousands. You see, about eight of those cows were just going to pay back the debt I owe him. So I've not much choice."

"Can we keep 'em until the end of the week?"

I'd spoken before I'd thought it through. Everyone was gawping at me.

"Any particular reason?" Mr Thomas asked.

"It's what you said about a fete, Gran."

"What about it?"

"Well, why don't we have one? Like a party to see off the cows."

Gran grinned at me. She seemed stuck for words for a moment, then she turned to Kate's dad. "We've no right to ask anything of you, Mr Thomas, after what we did, but I think that's a wonderful idea ... a proper fete with a stalls, a tombola, a raffle ... like in your father's day. It'd be a proper send-off."

Mr Thomas sighed. "I think my dad must have liked you."

"Oh, I was invisible to him," said Gran. "But I'll confess something to you – I had an almighty crush on him. I kept tabs on what he was up to after the war, and I bumped into him once. I could hardly speak. A month or two later I heard he was getting

married and I cried. He broke my heart without ever knowing it."

Gran smiled.

"What if I go and speak to Don Mostyn myself?" she said to Mr Thomas. "You never know ... if I tell him..."

"Gran. I already did."

"When? You never said."

"Yesterday. He's only interested in money. I probably made it worse – called him 'Miser Mostyn'. Sorry."

"Oh, Gemma," said Gran. "You shouldn't have."

Someone laughed. Mr Thomas was grinning at me.

He seemed different – sort of relaxed and kind. I glanced at Kate, who was smiling at me too. She had a lovely smile.

Forty Five

"What *is* a fete, Mam?"

I was so glad Darren asked, because I wasn't sure either. We were in the lounge working on the plan – everyone was getting into the idea.

"Well, it's ... it's a party, I suppose, in a way," said Mam. "Everyone enjoying a nice day outside with stalls and games. I remember the one we used to have on the Common, like your gran mentioned."

"Why did it stop?" I asked.

"I suppose the Mawr isn't the place it used to be," she said.

"What if it rains?"

"Maybe I can get the marquee from work."

"The what?" asked Darren.

"It's a big tent, love. We could have the stalls inside that if need be."

My phone rang. It was Kate.

"All right?"

"*Can you come to Cardiff with me?*" she asked.

"Mam, Kate wants me to go to Cardiff with her."

"What for?

"What for?" I asked Kate.

"*I'll tell you when I see you. S'important.*"

Kate paid for my ticket. So there I was, sat beside her on the bus. I was glad she asked me, but Kate was looking out the window as if I wasn't there. She seemed edgy.

"Karuna and Mr Banerjee are organising a Hindu thing, for the fete," I said, just for something to say. "Can't remember what it's called, but it celebrates spring, apparently. There'll be a tombola – which is like a raffle – Polly, Mrs Evans and Mave Rubens are doing that. Mrs Oleski and Mrs Choudary are doing cakes and hot drinks, and Roger's in charge of music. My mam's going to try and sort out a marquee ... a big tent..." I was going on, which was probably annoying and I couldn't bear the suspense, so I said, "Why we going to Cardiff?"

"To see Mr Phillips."

"Oh... Who's he?"

"He's the man from Defra who was checking over the cows. I thought he might be able to help with this." She gave me a piece of paper she'd printed off the Internet. It was all about kids visiting farms and learning about cows, pigs and everything.

"Looks good," I said, though I didn't know what it had to do with our cows.

"My dad's worried about what to do," said Kate.

"But he'll have the cows back after the fete," I said.

"It's not just that though. He feels bad about taking the cows off everyone."

"But they're his cows."

"I told him that. I told him. But he's upset about it now, and that's down to me. I made out it was all down to Mostyn putting pressure on him, but I knew it wasn't just that. There was no way out. Dad's desperate to do what's right. And it's all worse because of what I did..."

When I saw her tears that did it for me. I put my hand on her shoulder. "Listen. We'll go and see Clipboard Phillips. If he doesn't want to help we'll ... we'll smash up his office..." Kate looked at me. "Just

joking. We'll say we'll go to the papers..."

"No. I don't think—"

"Yeah, Kate! We'll go to the papers, tell them about the fete, and start a campaign, you know, like you see on the telly. We want the cows for the Bryn Mawr..." I glanced at the sheet of paper. "So that 'inner-city children, in particular, can gain an understanding of sustainable agri...culture and the invaluable contribution of farming and livestock'..."

"Livestock," said Kate.

"That's what I said."

"You said 'livstock'."

"Oh. '...the invaluable contribution of farming and *livestock* to all nations of the world ... including Wales'."

"Including Wales?"

"I added that bit."

Kate smiled. Job done.

When we got to Cardiff we walked until we got to this office-type building.

"This the place?" I asked.

She nodded – definitely nervous, she was.

"Come on then," I said, and led the way in.

There were two receptionists behind a long counter. One was busy and the other glanced at us and said, "Can I help?"

"We'd like to see Mr Phillips," said Kate.

"D'you have an appointment?"

"No."

"And you are?"

"Kate Thomas."

"And Gemma Matthews," I added, brushing my hair behind my ear. I wished I had a briefcase or something with me, just to look the business.

"Why d'you want to see him, exactly?"

"It's about the Bryn Mawr Dozen," I said.

"The what?"

"The cows on the Bryn Mawr."

She smiled. "Oh, yes."

I looked at Kate and winked.

"Mr Phillips?" said the receptionist into the phone. "I have Kate Thomas for you ... and a Gemma Matthews... No. She's here, in reception." Pause. "The Bryn Mawr cows..." Another pause. "Very well." She put the phone down. "Someone will be down directly."

"Thank you very much," I said to her, like I was totally with it.

I sat with Kate on these squeaky leather chairs while we waited. I tried to learn the printout Kate gave me, as I thought it might be useful. Then I noticed a yoghurt stain on my tracksuit top from

breakfast. I was trying to rub it off when a woman came up to us.

"Kate and Gemma? Would you follow me?"

She took us down corridors and through this big office with people at computers. They all looked at me and Kate as we went by. I nodded at them, like I was important, but at the same time wished I hadn't worn my jeans and tracksuit top with the yoghurt stain.

We were shown into a small office, and there was Mr Phillips, the man from Defra, 'cept he wasn't wearing his wellies.

The woman who took us there said, "Would you like a tea?"

"Yes, please," I said just as Kate said, "No, thank you." So I said, "Nah," coughed and crossed my legs.

"Right," said Mr Phillips. "What's this about?"

He didn't smile, which wasn't a good start.

"We want to start a City Farm on the Bryn Mawr," said Kate.

He looked at us like we'd said something rude. He opened his mouth to speak.

"So that inner-city children can understand anti... culture and livestock..." I said, but something came out wrong as he seemed well puzzled. "So that kids get to know about cows, basically."

Mr Phillips nodded slowly. “But I don’t see how I can help.”

I stood up. “Right! We’ll go to the papers then.”

Kate kicked me and I knew I’d put my foot in it.

FORTY SIX

I felt terrible on the bus going back. "Sorry, Kate."

"It's all right – he wasn't exactly gagging to help anyway."

"Why don't we go see Mostyn again?" I suggested.

Kate shook her head. "No. I don't want to make things any worse."

My phone rang. It was Mam.

"Hiya."

"*Just want you to know your dad's home.*"

"What, now?"

"*Yeah. Remember what I said – I want things nice and easy, Gemma. OK?*"

"Yes, Mam." Before I hung up I quickly said, "Loads of love."

"What's up?" Kate asked.

"My dad's home."

"For good?"

"Just the weekend. He'll be at the fete – you'll see him."

"I don't think I want to come to the fete."

"Why not?"

"Sorry, Gemma. I know you, Lilly and everyone are taking trouble to organise it an' all, but ... all those people and the cows, I just..."

"S'all right. I'm beginning to wish I hadn't thought of it now."

"No, it's a nice idea."

"No, honestly. I was thinking, we're going to have a big party and then the cows will be gone and everything will go back to how it was on the Mawr. What's to celebrate? It'll be the scuzzy place it always was. I don't want that. No one wants it."

We were quiet for the rest of the journey.

Dad was sitting in the lounge when I got in. Darren was sat next to him, grinning from ear to ear.

"All right, Gemma?" Dad said as he got up and gave me a hug. He seemed nervous, like he was worried

I'd have another go at him.

"All right," I said.

"Hey! Where's Tom Jones?" He was pointing at the sideboard.

I'd forgotten about the statue we'd smashed.

I glanced at Mam and Darren. "Sorry," I said. "It was—"

"Knocked him over dusting, I did," interrupted Mam. "Clumsy."

She winked at me.

"Oh, well. Ne'er mind," Dad mumbled, staring at the space where the statue used to be.

"Darren. Give us a hand," said Mam as she walked into the kitchen.

I reckon she did it deliberately, leaving me with Dad.

"It's good to be out," he said. "I mean, here."

He sat down at the table. "Well, well... Cows on the Mawr."

I was still standing and felt a bit awkward. "Not for much longer."

"What next, eh? Elephants?" He forced a laugh.

"We're having a fete tomorrow."

"Aye. Heard you're behind it?"

"Mam helped, and Gran, and Darren. Mr Banerjee and Karuna too." I was waiting for a reaction.

"There'll be a Hindu festival – a Holi. That's it! That's what Mr Banerjee called it."

"Smashing. Hear that, love?" he shouted towards the kitchen. "Holy fete."

"Holi, Dad – not holy."

Mam came to the doorway with Darren. "You going to go, Rob? There'll be a lot of eyes on you. A few comments too, no doubt."

"I'll stay here if it's going to be awkward for you."

"I don't mind," said Mam. "What about you, Darren?"

"I'll smash anyone who says anything nasty."

"Gemma?" asked Dad. "It's your party."

I glanced at Mam. I remembered about her saying she was always in, and making the most of Dad being here. "You got to face them some time, Dad," I said.

"You're right. I'll hide from no one – out in the open for all to see."

Like the cows, I thought, *before they're taken away.*

"Gemma."

Darren came up to me looking really serious.

"I found out who did it, Gem – who beat up Karuna."

"Who?"

"Tobin brothers. I heard them telling someone – laughing about it."

"Shouldn't we tell the police, Mam?" I said.

"Yeah, we should." She went over to the phone.

Dad stood up. "What are you doing?"

"Karuna was badly beaten up, Robbie," said Mam. "Right next door to Gran's."

"Listen. No son of mine's gonna be a grass."

Mam turned on him. "What! That what you learned inside, Robbie? It's OK to see someone beat up and leave it alone? Look away, is it? Let it go on and on – forever and ever?"

Dad's face went red. "What's got into you lot?" he said. "I come back and you're talking about cows and having a fete and ... and grassing on someone, just because them next door—"

"DON'T MAKE IT GO BACK, DAD!"

My voice filled the room like a lion.

"Don't make it go back to how it was, Dad, please. I love the way things are now, honest to God." I looked at Mam and Darren. "*We* love it. If you want it to go back to how it was, then..." I started to cry. "Then you might as well go back inside."

I ran upstairs.

I was lying on the bed in the dark when there was a knock at the door.

"Not now, Dad," I said. "Leave me alone, please."

"It's me, Gemma," said Darren. "Can I come in?"

That was the first time he'd ever asked.

He came in quietly and sat on the end of my bed. "Mam's called the police," he said. "They're coming to ask me some questions."

I sat up. "Good."

"I'm worried, Gem. I don't want to be a grass."

"What's a grass, Darren?"

"You know – someone who tells on someone."

"And why is it bad?"

He shrugged. "Just is. No one likes a grass."

"Darren, what if the Tobin brothers had attacked me? Or Mam? Or your gran? What then?"

"But..."

"But it's OK if they beat up someone else. Is that it?"

He sighed. "No. Course not, but what if I get called a grass by kids?"

"You tell 'em cows love grass."

He smiled. I put my arm around his shoulder. "If someone lays a finger on you, Darren, you promise to tell me, yeah?"

He nodded. "What would you do, Gem?"

"I'll tell 'em what you did was right. Then I'll send Kate round."

He grinned.

"What's Dad doing?"

"He's all quiet. Come downstairs, Gem. I want you to be there when the police get here."

My brother was asking me to be with him – after that nothing was going to surprise me.

"Come on then."

Forty Seven

We were up at the crack of dawn with tons to do.

Dad wasn't down, as he was having a lie-in, but to be honest I was glad he stayed in bed as I wanted to concentrate on the fete and everything. Me and Mam's mobiles were ringing non-stop. Then Mam said, "Right! We're gonna sit down and have a proper breakfast, cos we'll need it. I'm putting these phones in the fridge so we can have some peace."

She did, too. Me and Darren laughed. It was while we were taking the breakfast things through that I had this funny thought. I was carrying the carton of milk, and as I put it on the table I said, "Mam. How

much milk do we use in a day?"

"One of those easy," she replied.

As I poured the milk in my bowl of cereal I was thinking that a litre was a lot just between me, Darren and Mam.

"D'you reckon we could do without milk, Mam?"

"Oh Gemma! C'mon. A drop of milk isn't going to—"

"No, Mam. I wasn't having a go, honest. But it would be difficult for all of us, wouldn't it? No cereal or cups of tea or coffee, or milk for cooking."

"Well, some people use soya milk," she said.

"Vomit," said Darren. "I want proper milk."

"I'm not saying we shouldn't have milk, I'm not."

I didn't know why I suddenly felt upset, but I couldn't get the thought of milk out of my head. It was a bit weird.

"What is it, love?" Mam asked.

"*I love milk,*" I said into the megaphone.

The marquee was in front of me. It was big enough for all the stalls to fit inside, so that people could drift in and out. There were loads of people, masses of them. In the middle of the Common were the thirteen cows. Donna's new calf was the star attraction, but then she was the cutest thing you ever saw. The music was faded out and everyone had come to a standstill when Gran had spoken to them through the megaphone.

When she handed it to me I was absolutely bricking myself.

I swallowed. "*I love milk...*" I said again. "*I had milk this morning. So did my brother, and my mam and dad...*" It sounded stupid, but I couldn't stop now. Mam smiled and gave me a nod of encouragement. "*I sat there thinking about milk. Everyone on the Mawr would have milk on their table, same as me. All the supermarkets would have their shelves stacked up with milk cartons – all different sizes. There's two supermarkets just on the Mawr alone, plus all the shops that sell milk. And apparently, the milk in cartons would've been in a cow only one or two days before. I wonder how many cartons of milk there are in Wales right now, in shops and fridges at home, and I wonder how many in Britain? Millions and millions, I suppose. Kate told me that farmers like Mr Thomas only get about a third of the price we pay for a litre. Not much, is it? It's cheap, when you think what you can do with milk. But the thing is, all the milk, everywhere in the world, all comes from cows like Jane. Millions of cows giving up millions of litres of their milk, just for us...*"

They stared at me in silence.

"When I looked at that carton of milk this morning I thought about cows... They haven't a clue how much we need their milk, and all they want is grass. It's mad when you think about it. Grass is everywhere. We're standing on it, and like my brother Darren said, you put grass in one end of a cow and milk comes out the other. It's like magic. Well, it is magic! Anyway, I told my mam this at breakfast this morning, and she told Gran who asked me to tell you..."

Everyone was looking at me, like they were waiting for the point, but that was it. That was all I thought at the breakfast table. I handed the megaphone back to Gran, and then they all started clapping. Well embarrassed, I was, and pleased at the same time. I saw Mam grinning, and then I noticed Dad beside her. It was odd seeing him there. I suppose it was because I hadn't seen him outside, as it were, for ages. There he was, stood among all the people, smiling at me but looking lost.

I went over to him. "Hi, Dad!" I said as cheerily as I could.

"Lovely speech, girl," he said. "Proud of you, I am."

"You tasted Gran's cheese yet?"

"No."

"Come on then."

I took him over to Gran in the tent, where loads of people were trying her cheese and butter. "Welcome home, Robbie," she said.

Dad nodded. "Thanks, Lilly."

"Hello, Robbie!" Roger said. "Let you out, did they? Or did you saw through the bars?"

"Roger!" Mam snapped.

"It's all right, Claire," said Dad. "Just having a joke, weren't you, Rodge?"

Roger looked embarrassed. "Course I was."

Drums started beating and bells were ringing – the Holi festival had begun. Three huge kites rose up with multicoloured tails hanging down. People were throwing coloured powder into the sky. It was wild, like a rainbow exploding. I ended up with yellow and red in my hair, and on my clothes. It made it seem like a proper festival, a festival for the cows. Everyone seemed to be having a good time, but I wished Kate was there to see it all, even if it made her sad knowing the cows would be sold. I noticed Karuna was controlling one of the kites, pulling at the line as he moved backwards.

"Gemma," he called.

As he came level with me he said, "I wanted to thank you, your mother and your brother."

"What for?"

"The police came and took fingerprints off my flute. Some were not mine, and they think they may belong to the boys that attacked me and tried to take it."

"Good."

"And we should all thank you for this – the fete."

I shrugged and could feel my cheeks getting warm.

"D'you want to hold the kite?"

"Go on then."

He handed me the ball of string. "Be careful – it's windy."

As soon as I took it I could feel the power of the wind, pulling at me, like the kite wanted to get away and fly on its own. As I watched it high up in the sky, the tail making a rattling sound in the wind, I forgot about all that was going on – all the upset and worry. I forgot the cows would have to be taken away. For a moment I was happy watching that kite moving back and forth. I glanced down to see if Mam was watching and noticed that Dad was gone.

"Where's Dad?" I called out to her.

"It's a bit much for him, love," she said. "He's gone back home."

She smiled, but I could tell she was upset. I didn't like the thought of Dad on his own, so I handed the kite back to Karuna. "I've got to go, sorry."

Forty Eight

I expected Dad to be lying on the settee watching TV when I got in, but the house was quiet. I thought he was having a nap until I went through to the kitchen and there he was, sitting with his back to me.

He turned with a start. "Gemma! You shocked the living—"

"Sorry, Dad."

"Why are you covered in paint?"

I must have looked freaky. "It's Hindu Holi – celebrating spring."

"Oh... What you doing back so early?"

"Didn't fancy staying. Too many people." It wasn't

the truth but I didn't want him to tell me to go back. I flicked on the kettle. "Want a cup of tea? I'm gasping."

"Yes, please, though I could have made one myself."

"S'all right."

"No, it's weird, Gemma. See, inside... In prison, everything's done for you. Might sound good, but I was sitting here and it didn't cross my mind that I could get up and make a cup of tea."

"Don't you have a kettle in the ... in the room?"

"Aye, and a TV and my own key to the door." He laughed.

"Don't joke!" I snapped. The anger came back, full force. "Whenever we visited we always asked how you were, and you'd make jokes, but you never asked how *we* felt having you inside. We never went anywhere or did anything, Dad, because we couldn't afford to. You made *us* prisoners."

The kettle boiled and clicked off. The steam twirled up to the ceiling like it was my anger escaping. For the first time I can remember, Dad was serious; but not just serious, he seemed sad.

"You're right, Gem. I made things bad for you all, but that doesn't mean I didn't think about you every day. I knew your mam was struggling, course I did, but I didn't want to think about that, 'specially after your gran visited."

"Gran? When did she visit?"

"Not long after I went in. Had a proper go at me. She put me straight, all right, but I couldn't bear the real picture. So I thought about a happy, made-up family to stop myself going crazy. I thought about us going on a picnic – just the four of us. I borrowed a car from a mate and we drove to a place I used to cycle to as a kid..."

I clenched my jaw shut. Dad stared out the window as he spoke. "The sun was shining and there was a waterfall and we sat under a tree and ate the food. Me and Darren stuck our heads in the water. God, it was cold." He smiled to himself. "Lovely, that day was. The times I thought about it."

"It wasn't made up though, Dad," I said.

"I didn't think you'd remember. It was a long time ago."

"When you put your heads in the waterfall Darren said it froze his brain..."

Dad laughed. "That's right."

"You wore a checked shirt, short sleeves. You'd just bought it, and a cowboy hat. You'd done a house clearance with your mate Danny, and with the money you bought Mam a dress, and the shirt and hat for yourself. You bought me new shoes – pretty

red sandals with a flower on the strap, and you bought Darren a cowboy outfit..."

Tears were rolling down my cheeks – a mini waterfall.

"I remember you tried to teach me and Darren to do handstands, and during the picnic Mam screamed because a wasp was on her. You said the wasp had good taste. After the picnic you climbed the massive tree. Darren wanted to follow but he couldn't reach the first branch. Mam shouted for you to come down, scared you'd break your neck. You went up so high... You're right, Dad. It was a lovely day."

He had a peculiar look on his face as I remembered those things. He put his hand on mine. "We'll go back there, love. I promise. We'll have a special day out."

"No. Somewhere else, Dad," I said. "Seaside would be nice ... but don't wear the cowboy hat."

"You're on!"

His smile faded quickly. "I phoned someone earlier – did a bit of digging around. I found out the police brought the Tobin boys in for questioning. Seems they found one of the brother's fingerprints on that boy's flute. It was wrong what I said last night. I suppose I was a bit thrown. See, you've all changed so much – your mam, Darren and 'specially you. I feel left behind in a way ... and stupid, that's the thing. I feel stupid."

"You're not stupid, Dad."

He nodded. "Clever man goes to prison, dumps his family in it and tells son not to go to the police with information on an assault... Oh Gemma, I'm a complete idiot." He clenched his fist and made it go white. He pressed his lips together, then gasped as he breathed in deeply. "Gonna try this time, Gemma," he said. "I mean it. I'll get a job, even if I have to go to Cardiff. Whatever it takes. I don't want to go back there. Ever."

"And we don't want you to."

I put my hand on his clenched fist. It opened and I took his hand. "Come back to the fete with me, Dad."

"I can't, Gem." He glanced down. "Scared."

"It's OK to feel scared, Dad. Come on. Come be with Mam. She's always on her own."

He got to his feet, and I led him out.

FORTY NINE

I didn't get as far as the farmhouse, because I found Kate sitting on the gate gazing out at the empty field where the cows used to be. As soon as she saw me she smiled, and I thought it was funny that it wasn't long ago I'd been scared of her.

"All right?" I said.

"Yeah. Why you covered in paint?"

"Spring is here."

"Huh?"

I went over and leaned on the gate next to her. "They named Donna's new calf Kate," I said.

"That's nice."

"You should see it down there. Loads of people... Wish you'd come down."

Kate didn't answer. She just stared out into the field, as if she could see cows.

"How's your dad?" I asked.

"Not great. He's going to take the cows to market and get 'em sold. It'll cost a lot to get 'em there, and he still feels bad about taking them away from everyone."

"Donna and Kate too?"

She nodded. "He and Mam helped me apply for the City Farm grant. Mr Phillips called Dad, said it was a good idea but he couldn't help as he works for Defra, like he told us."

"But the cows would be sold by the time you got the grant, wouldn't they?"

"Yeah. I think they helped me apply just to please me... How's *your* dad?" she asked.

"It's weird having him back. He doesn't like being outside, with all the people and everything."

Kate took a deep breath. "We should go down and bring up the cows. No point leaving it any longer."

"You got a bike?"

"No."

"I'll take you down. Be quicker."

"No."

"Why?"

"I can't ride a bike. All right!"

It was the old angry Kate, her eyes back to narrow slits.

"Don't you dare laugh, Gemma."

"I'm not laughing. You don't have to ride it – I can cycle with you on the saddle."

"No!"

My phone started ringing. It was Mam.

"Hiya."

"*We're bringing the cows up now, Gemma...*"

"We're just about to come down..."

"*It's OK, love, we can manage. Don't worry.*"

She was gone.

"They're bringing the cows up."

Kate nodded. "No need to go down on your bike then."

She walked to the end of the lane and I followed, trying to wipe the smile off my face.

We gazed down on the Bryn Mawr below. It was a lovely view.

"You ever had a pet?" Kate asked.

"Had a goldfish once. Won it at a fair ... or maybe it was a fete."

"Goldfish's not a proper pet. It's a fish!"

"Still a pet."

"What happened to it?"

"Darren put Slush Puppy in the bowl – killed it."

As we looked down I saw the colourful kites.

"Hey, there's the..."

Then I saw something else. I couldn't work it out at first, it was like some sort of creature moving up the hill towards us. I'll never ever forget it.

The kites were leading the way, and the cows were plodding along behind. Then after the cows were people, hundreds and hundreds of people, thousands, all following them. It was like everyone in the whole of the Bryn Mawr had decided to take a stroll at the same time – a massive parade to see the cows off.

Me and Kate watched in silence.

"You don't think they're coming all the way up, do you?" I asked.

Kate glanced at me, and then back down at the procession snaking its way up Craig-y-Nos hill. "Hope they don't expect a cup of tea."

When we got to the farmhouse I don't think Kate's dad and mam believed us.

It was bizarre when the people arrived, because some of them were covered in coloured paint that made them look like a wild war party. They all just

stood there, looking at us, and they were just the first part of the crowd. The rest were still coming.

I noticed lots of them were carrying milk cartons. They came towards us, put the cartons on the floor, and then they turned and walked away. No one said a word. It was a bit spooky.

I picked up one of the cartons. It was heavy but it didn't have milk in it.

"It's full of money," I said to Kate. "They're *all* full of money."

It took over an hour for the people to come and give their milk cartons, but it wasn't just people from the Mawr; they were from all over the Valleys.

Me, Dad, Mam and Darren helped stack up the cartons in the milking shed. Kerry said it was an irony, putting them in there.

One of the other things about that day I'll not forget was when I saw Sian standing there. She put a carton on the floor and looked at me. She didn't smile, just gave me a nod. I nodded back, then she turned and left.

It took a few days before we got through counting the money. It kept coming, too. People sent donations to the *Echo* from all over Wales. There was plenty to pay Mr Thomas for at least six of the cows – half a dozen to start the Bryn Mawr City Farm.

FIFTY

We raised so much money in the end we bought all thirteen cows, and we got the grant for the farm as well.

The first thing we did was to clear the Mawr Common of rubbish. We had loads of help. The cows were allowed to graze, and we helped Mr Thomas put a fence all the way round the Common. Even Mostyn gave a hand – amazing what happens with a bit of publicity. Me and Kate became the first members of the BMCF – the Bryn Mawr City Farm – and Mr Thomas was the manager.

Mr Banerjee and his family suggested we marked

the opening with a procession of the cows decorated with flowers and coloured blankets. It was great. People shared gifts and food. Peggy led the procession and someone was carried high on a chair, dressed in white with a crown of jewels. It was only when the person started to play the flute that I realised it was Karuna. His face and body was painted blue – I know I keep saying it, but he was gorgeous.

I said to Mr Banerjee. "Is he meant to be Krishna?"

He smiled. "Yes. The holy herdsman."

When the music stopped there were lots of people gathered around Karuna, mostly girls. I remembered Mr Banerjee telling me about the cow maids fancying Krishna. I felt jealous.

I spotted Kate, hiding behind her mam and dad. It was funny, her not liking to be around loads of people. I'd always thought nothing bothered her, but she stood there looking like a shy toddler. I went over to her.

"Hi."

She smiled. "Hi."

We gazed around at all that was going on, and I couldn't help thinking that it was all because of me and her. "Good, isn't it?" I said.

She nodded.

"You doing anything tomorrow?" I asked.

"No."

"I'll come up and see you."

"OK," she said.

"I'll bring my bike – give you your first lesson."

I didn't wait for a reply and went over to where Darren was being interviewed by the TV people.

"Tell us what's so special about Jane?" the reporter asked.

"Well, we get milk from her, and butter and cheese..." said Darren, staring into the camera like he was in a trance. "And you can't say that about a cat or a dog or a hamster, can you? A cow's loads better." He pointed to Jane. "Chewing the cud, she is now. Cows bring back up the grass they've eaten and chew it again. Fantastic. Imagine if you could eat a Mars bar, then bring it up and eat it again and again..."

I laughed.

Dad was out of prison now and I knew he still found it difficult being among lots of people. When I spotted him he looked like he wanted to be a hundred miles away – something he had in common with Kate. As I went towards him I saw him take Mam's hand. A lump filled my throat. I turned away and walked around on my own for a bit.

I felt like I was in a different place, not the Mawr I remembered – a happy place, with people chatting

and laughing.

"Hello, Gemma."

I turned to see Karuna. He really *was* blue – bizarre but gorgeous.

"Fantastic, isn't it?" he said. "And all because of you and Kate."

I shrugged. "We did our best." Like it was every week I helped rescue twelve cows. "When can we have another flute lesson?" I asked him straight out. Cool, I was.

"Tonight?"

"OK," I said with a smile. Then I kissed him on his blue lips.

Audacious, or what?

"Come meet my mam and dad," I said to him.

As we made our way around the fete we stopped to watch Gran talking to people and sharing her cheese. She was so happy. I remembered the day she was miserable in the rain burying her dog, and now she was standing in the sunshine talking to people about her cow and her cheese.

It was beautiful, just beautiful.

Fifty One

Kate was frowning, and she gripped the handlebars like her life depended on it.

"You let go and I'll—"

"I won't," I said. "As you move you'll balance. It's automatic. Honest."

"Doesn't feel automatic."

We were on a quiet lane, down the road from the farm, because Kate didn't want her parents to know she was learning to cycle.

"OK. Feet on pedals."

Kate's arms were shaking. "Don't let go!"

"I won't."

"If you do..."

"I WON'T!"

We started going along. Then I heard a noise, like a whirring sound. A cyclist was coming down the lane on a proper speed-bike, all kitted out in Lycra and a helmet. There was a whoosh as the cyclist went past.

"Wow!"

I let go of the bike. I didn't mean to.

"GEMMA!"

Before I could get to her, Kate went straight into the hedge at the side of the lane. She never believed I let go by accident, but she'd cycled and that was the main thing. From then on we went cycling most weekends. We even went down Craig-y-Nos hill together, no brakes.

We screamed all the way down.

Cowgirls screaming for our lives.

Acknowledgements

At the top of the list of people who have been instrumental in helping me get *Cowgirl* published is my agent, Claire Wilson, at Rogers, Coleridge and White Ltd. She was alone in being "intrigued" to see the rest of the book when I found myself back to square one. If it wasn't for her subsequent editing, encouragement and representation, *Cowgirl* would only be a file on my computer, long unopened.

Kate Wilson and Nosy Crow were brave enough to take it on board. Their enthusiasm and support made me feel part of a great team. Kirsty Stansfield's precise and intelligent editing made the book whole, and I'd also like to thank Adrian Soar and others for their feedback.

From the time I properly challenged myself to become a writer I have had kind employers who accommodated my need for "time off to write" – so grateful thanks to Waltham Forest Mencap, the Gloucestershire Social Services Adoption Support Team, Woodside Primary School in London and, especially, The Care Forum in Bristol.

A big thank you to Karen Barnes and the boys and girls at Winchcombe School, Gloucestershire, for their time and feedback in testing early material, and equally to Angela Depper for reading my writing to children at the Croft Preparatory School in Stratford-upon-Avon. It was all above and beyond your call of duty.

Many moons ago I was fortunate to have the generous advice and time of the author Susan Price. I'd also like to thank the tutors Julia Green, Steve Voake, John McLay and Lucy Christopher at Bath Spa University, as well as Amy Wigelsworth, Peter Buckman and Anne-Marie Doulton.

A special thank you to Dave Wood for helping a troubled boy untie a hefty "ball of knots".

In writing *Cowgirl* I am indebted for the help of Janatha Stout, Head of Agriculture at Hartpury College, Gloucestershire, as well as John Womack in Somerset for their knowledge of farming and dairy production. Jonathan Crump gave me a guided tour of Wick Court Farm for City Children and showed me his Gloucestershire cheese (single and double) being made. Thanks also to Richard Jones and Adrian Rogers at Defra.

In researching Hinduism I'm grateful to Judit Bajusz and the Oxford Centre for Hindu Studies in helping me with fine details, and thanks also to Ruby Dass.

Friends and family have been supportive over a number of years and in a number of ways. So heartfelt thanks to: Caroline Adams, Vittorio, Marco and Alex Baratto, Havva Basto, Caroline Beale, Matt Blandford, Julian Bloom, Sophie Brown, Frankie, Andy, Molly and Billy Campbell (Sid & Otto for always bringing the ball back), Simon Campbell, Sharon Thomas, Felix and Rosa, Simon Cooke, Samantha Cordwell, Grace and Michael Dembowicz, Chris Dickens and Clio David, Pamela Gemin, Colin Hutton, Fabienne Illiano, Damien and Andrew James, Tatjana Lisson, Danielle Oldacre, Annie Peutrel, Liz Pickering, Kate Pitt and Janet Wallis.

A special mention to Neil Bastian and Andy Ward, who know what it takes and have shared many hours with me chewing the cud.

Finally, to Isabelle Endreo for your love and support, even while you were facing serious illness.